IRON MAIDENS

Sarah Jane Huntington

CONTENTS

INTRODUCTION

Like many women, I grew up on a steady diet of deliciously frightening horror movies. One thing I hated was the portrayal of the female.

Too many movies featured a perfectly slim, beautiful woman standing screaming, falling over, or taking her top off. Just purely there for show. All weak, all afraid.

I knew women weren't like that. I knew we came in all kinds of beautiful shapes and sizes. I knew we were strong and fierce.

Women don't always need to be the final girl, sometimes, they can be the villain too.

Women can do anything a man can do and more.

Maybe, just maybe, we are better at hiding our dark sides… I know I am (cue evil laugh).

One last note: *Gods and Monsters* was adapted from a story *The Void* in my first book, *Paint It Black*. The theme seemed too good to not play around with.

HEADACHES

I have a story to tell you, and by the end of it, I might understand if you hate me. You might cross the street to avoid me, or you might run in the opposite direction entirely. I don't mind. Truth is, I don't care how you feel.

My tale is about darkness, rage, and surviving. Survival means different things to different people. I get that, but this is *my* story, my survival. Just mine.

Something happened to me. Maybe it was karma, maybe it was a fat dose of '*Serves you right.*' I was certainly due, I guess.

Maybe my affliction is my body standing up for itself and acting against me, or then again, acting *for* me…

My mind feels full of crawling insects, stinging nasty wasps, and the hiss of television static. I often wonder if razor blades and sharp glass sit in place of a brain in my skull, all kept together and bound with thick barbed wire. No cells, no neurons, just black rot and decay.

I was born angry. A ball of fury in a tiny female body.

A meanness grew to live in the marrow of my bones and in me, it latched on and thrived. I was sullen, bitter, unremorseful. I never smiled, I sneered instead.

I had contempt for everything except myself.

My Ma used to tell us all that old cliche story. She said everyone had two bears inside them. She told us that the one we fed the most would be the one we eventually became.

She was a liar, or just plain wrong.

I was born with one bear. The good one was missing entirely.

I knew it and Ma soon knew it too. We could both sense the hollowness inside me.

She called me vile, selfish. She claimed I was her greatest mistake. Obviously, we were never close.

As I aged, anger ate away at any good parts of me that might be hidden underneath the layers of hate, like a tiny Pac-man chomping away. I despised the world and everyone in it, and my view only declined.

Life was intolerable.

I grew up in a house jammed full of five other loud girls and two even louder boys. That was no easy feat, believe me.

Our Ma knocked out children as if she were a cat with a litter of kittens, while my father, the dirty tomcat, ran for the hills in despair.

From dawn until the night came, the sounds of the house would be suffocating and unbearable. Eight children of various ages, all vying for attention.

I struggled to be seen or heard above the needs of my siblings. I went in for the kill as soon as I had someone's eyes on me. I could turn a single-line story into a long, very tiresome book, and I never knew when to quit. If anyone got bored of me, I would pinch them hard or clamp my teeth down on their tender arm. That trick always got them looking at me again.

Violence, it seemed, could be the answer after all.

I grew out of that behavior eventually, kind of, after my eldest sister Emma fell out of our attic window. She went plummeting to the ground, limbs twisting and flailing like an old rag doll. Instead of old stuffing falling out, it was her bloody innards that got strewn about the lawn. She landed on a particularly sharp piece of solid wood fencing. Staked, skewered. Arms and legs twitched as blood erupted from her mouth.

Suspicion fell on me.

After all, I was in the attic with her when she fell. I copied the expressions of my siblings, cried with borrowed tears until I was in the clear.

Still, after that, I was largely avoided. No one liked me, me with my darkness and anger.

People whispered about me, only narrowed eyes ever landed on me.

I decided to become someone new. A mask to shape and wear, an illusion of nice.

I tried and failed to be the strong silent type; I think I lacked the inner calm to pull it off. Whenever I tried to stare thoughtfully off into the distance, people around me figured I might be having a stroke.

I tried to be a sweet girly type, but I repulsed myself within an hour. I hadn't been able to be the smiley witty type on account of the fact that I was the least funny person I knew.

I only laughed when people fell over and hurt themselves. I found that hilarious.

Finally, I settled on being a moody and intolerable tomboy. I liked to watch people. Especially when they think they're alone. Only then do you get to see the real person underneath the mask they wear in public. So, I became a moody watcher.

I had Ma cut my long blonde hair short; I dyed it black, and I stuck to it.

The last thing my ma ever called me was a killer and a murderer. She was right. Guilty as charged.

I should start at the beginning, but it's difficult now. I feel as if everything started way before I knew about it or even before I even suspected what was happening.

Memories are a fickle thing. We keep them boxed up like old records and hidden away in the fleshy pink neurons and whatnots of our brain's storage areas. Sometimes, I imagine I have an old wooden rocking chair in my head. I use it to sit on when I need to recall memories. I play them on a screen inside my head while I watch the images flicker.

Every so often, one of my memories gets brought out of my brain's filing cabinet. I have to blow the metaphorical dust away by thinking hard on it, just to get it to play again. Often, they are too frayed to play at all. I throw those ones away.

As far as I recall, everything occurred in roughly this sequence of events.

I first started having headaches a couple of weeks after I was released from prison. Prison itself wasn't so bad for me. I wasn't anyone's bitch, and I enjoyed the freedom in the structure and order. I didn't have to think for myself; I was guaranteed food every day, and I had a roof over my head.

I made a few friends there, not from wanting any, but out of the necessity to survive the often harsh environment. My cellmate died, but that wasn't a shame at all. She was a snorer, a loud one too.

I learned a lot from watching the women around me, enough so that I could mirror their actions for my own future use, to better play at being a regular woman. I copied body language, facial expressions, words, and phrases. Anything I thought might serve a use to me when I was released back into the society I wasn't welcome to be a part of.

I'd been serving two years after being caught drink driving, although I surely deserved more.

I fell out of my car when they pulled me over on an empty stretch of road, veins full of vodka, and my jeans splattered with vomit. I hardly needed to be breathalyzed.

What they didn't know is that the drunk driving bit happened on the way back from a different crime scene entirely.

When I get to that part, you might understand the drinking bit a little better.

I went to see a kindly grey-haired doctor for my headaches; she prescribed pills to help with the crippling pain. Pills that didn't work. I went back, angry and demanding. Something was changing inside me, and I knew it. The rage that had a home in me twisted and writhed. It expanded and threatened to overwhelm me or explode. My bad bear was rising.

I had no idea how to explain any of it. I was never good with feelings. But I was worried *for myself*. I didn't want to get caught doing something the law said I shouldn't be doing and end up back in prison. I wanted my freedom. Also, I did not want to die.

Self-preservation was always high on my list of priorities.

"The headaches could be stress-related. Have you tried therapy?" The doctor asked.

Nope, and I won't. I can't risk anyone peeling back the layers and finding the real me buried underneath, I thought.

"No, I want a scan or something. I'm worried."

She agreed, and I was booked in for tests for three weeks.

Tests I didn't show up for.

I couldn't you see, not by then.

A small lump had started to grow, tender and sore at first, right on the back of my head, underneath the tight skin of my skull. I felt it emerge before it came into existence.

My stupid new boyfriend Eric, a useless idiot but with his own nice apartment I wouldn't leave, suspected I had a tumor.

Eric was pretty to look at, that was all. I picked him up in a dive of a bar, lured him with sexual promises I couldn't be bothered to perform. Still, he had his uses.

The lump soon got bigger and began to form in shape with peculiar little hard ridges around the edges.

I did what I always do whenever I had a problem: I ignored it.

Around a week or so later, I walked into an empty diner to kill time and to spend more of Eric's money. I ordered a full-cooked breakfast, and I couldn't remember eating it.

I woke from my daze and saw the licked-clean plate sitting in front of me. I noticed the two diner staff looking at me with disgusted horror.

"What are you looking at?" I yelled. "Piss off."

What did I do? Shit, leave!

I swallowed my anger and vague thoughts that I might have had a blackout. I left quickly and refused to think about it.

I was lost in a daydream, that's all. And I ate greedily. That's why they were staring. Just forget about it.

I went straight to buy donuts in a different diner and sat enjoying them all. Then I bought fat juicy burgers from one of those street stalls. I had never felt so viciously hungry.

***

Two days later, on an ordinary dull Wednesday night, Eric brought home a delicious large box of fried chicken. My job was simple: I was to divide it all up while he took a shower. When he came back in, the whole lot was gone, bones and all.

Needless to say, he wasn't happy with me, and I was baffled. He left to fetch more. He took his keys and tutted as he left. He didn't dare push me, not with my temper. Anger was never far away, it bubbled under the surface of my carefully constructed mask like lava.

I knew I must have eaten the food, but I couldn't for the life of me taste it, or even remember it. That was a real shame because fried chicken had always been my favorite.

The next day, I asked Eric to peer underneath my hair again. My headache felt so bad, and my lump tingled and itched until it burned.

"Annie," he gasped. "This is so weird. It's got, I don't know… White bits, wait! Is that bone?"

"Idiot," I snapped. "Course it's not bone."

Is it?

I slapped his hands away and wondered if he had lost his usefulness.

Friday, that same week, I woke up with no headache for the first time in months. For a blissful few seconds, I relished the feel of having no relentless throbbing pain.

The curtains were open, the sun was shining on me. I felt warm and cozy.

I stretched out on the bed and felt sticky dampness underneath my hands.

My eyes flew open, and I saw the cheap sheets we slept on were covered in blood, and I mean covered, drenched in fact. I frantically checked myself all over, convinced I was bleeding to death before I realized the blood wasn't even mine.

I felt angry over the mess and furious at Eric for leaving me with it.

"ERIC!" I yelled. No answer.

I searched the apartment for him, I checked the linen cupboard and I even looked under the sink, but I found no trace of his stupid self. I called him and followed the sound. His phone sat by the bedside table jingling its happy tune. No Eric anywhere. Only his watch, bloody and gore-splattered, lay on the cheap carpet.

So, I did what I do when I have a problem and I can't ignore it, I ran.

I didn't care about him, or what had happened to him. I was worried about myself.

Did I do something? Was it me? But where's the body? A hundred questions tumbled over each other in my mind.

I figured he might have been injured and gone to the hospital somehow. I didn't want to be stuck looking after him when he returned. That wasn't something I was capable of, caring.

I showered and packed my few things into a backpack. I stole Eric's cards and cash and I bolted. I refused to think. Refused entirely.

I was always good at that. Whatever happened in my life, I'd take the memory off to storage in my brain and lock it firmly away.

Out of sight, out of mind.

I withdrew as much as I could from the nearest machine and sought out a bathroom in a diner. I had a mirror in my bag, a little compact. I angled it over the grimy bathroom mirror to peer at the back of my head. I had a huge lump. Fleshy pink with a thick line running down the middle. It looked utterly disgusting. Little ridges and white bits caught the light. The inside looked as if it was sinking in somehow.

Some kind of brain-eating bacteria? A parasite? This is impossible! What is it? Am I going to die? Calm down, it's just a...

A woman came in and stared at me. "What?" I snapped. Fury bubbled up inside me. I wanted her to provoke me, to say something, anything.

She glided past me and into a cubicle. I left and caught the first Greyhound bus out of dodge.

I knew where I was going. I always heard people say that a person shouldn't burn their bridges. I only had two bridges, and I hadn't set fire to either.

In prison, I had a favorite of all the women. Grace. I didn't like her, not in any way. My fake persona, and her real one, made friends.

When she left, she gave me the offer to visit her, to look her up if I ever needed a place to stay. I had her address written in jagged pencil on a single piece of paper. I knew she lived in a trailer, I knew she'd been inside for fraud, a relatively tame crime.

My plan was to stay with her for a few days so I could think.

It took half a day to get there on a coach full of sweaty neurotic people. I stared out of the window and watched the world go by. All the normal people with their empty lives, going home to watch soap operas and stupid reality television with their equally dull families.

I felt separated from people like that. Most, I imagined, had good bears inside them. That, it seemed, made all the difference in life.

Did I resent others? I don't know, but nor did I care.

A fire burned in me. I couldn't wait to get off the bus. The sounds all those people made on the journey felt relentless. Each one frayed my nerves until I felt flames spark in my bones.

Finally, we arrived. I pushed past everyone to get off first. My bag crashed into faces and bodies.

"Hey! Watch out!" A guy with a beard yelled at me.

I elbowed him hard. "Fucking try me," I seethed. "I dare you."

His eyes widened, his mouth went slack. How I loved looks like those.

He stepped back, and I felt a surge of power inside me. Almost like an electric shock of bliss. I could smell him, his sudden fear. The scent made me hungry. I was above him, better than him. He was nothing.

People like him, they always think they're the dominant ones. Fools.

I smiled and winked. I climbed off the bus spitefully slowly.

I headed straight to buy food.

An hour later, I knocked at the trailer door. Grace's home. It was a tired-looking, small trailer, with a few dead plants rotting in pots outside. I knocked three times.

"Annie!" she cried as she swung the door open. The first thing I saw was her black eye. Bruises trailed along her throat and collarbone. She looked thin, tired, and sick. Her hair was a different color. In prison, it had been blonde. She'd dyed it an awful red. The loud color matched her eyes.

"Come in! I'm so glad you came, I hoped you would! How are you? When did you get out?"

My mind struggled to focus and spasmed. "I'm fine," was all I managed to say. "What happened to your face?"

Straight to the point. Blunt. I had no other way I could be.

Grace went deathly quiet. Without warning, she put her head in her hands and started crying. I felt uncomfortable straight away. I looked around her small trailer. It looked quite nice inside, cozy and clean. Two small chairs sat opposite each other. I dropped my pack and sat down.

Shit, now what? What do I do?

I remembered. Recalled exactly what I had seen other women do.

"There, there," I said and patted her hand. "Tell me all about it. Tell me everything."

She did. Once she spat one word out, the rest came tumbling free. I was soon bored and cracked open her whiskey bottle.

It turned out Grace had herself a nasty boyfriend. A drunk and predictably, one with a temper. He lived at the edge of the very same trailer park. Greg was his name.

She told me all about him, in great detail. So much so that I even knew the size and width of his tiny, disappointing penis. He sounded like a little boy in a man's body and nothing more.

My nature is different from most. I appreciate that. Still, I despise men bullying women, hitting those weaker than themselves.

They do it, I think, to feel better about themselves. To feel greater than they are. But they are not. They are very far from better, the furthest thing from greater. They are filth.

A superior predator preys not on the weak, but on the strong. I know that.

I couldn't wait to meet Greg. As soon as Grace passed out from drinking whiskey shots, I snuck out.

I only wanted to get a look at him. Just a small look, a little assessment.

I went unarmed. Just me and I knocked on his door three times.

"Hello pretty," he greeted me. "I haven't seen you before."

Corny bastard.

"Hi," I smiled. I fluttered my eyelashes and giggled. A moronic sound, but one that always worked well. "I'm new here."

"Welcome to the park. Do you want to come in and have a beer?"

"Oh!" I laughed. "Isn't your girlfriend or wife home?"

"Nah. I'm single!"

Liar, liar, pants on fire.

And so easy. Always so very easy.

I'm small, thin, and kind of pretty if you squint hard enough. I look cheap, trashy. I look fun and up for anything. I am underestimated. I depend on that.

Only a close look at my dead doll eyes could reveal anything of my real nature. Greg, stupid Greg, he was too busy staring at my chest to peer at my face. I stepped inside.

As soon as the door shut on us, I found myself standing by a sink. In the sink was a shiny, big knife covered in melted cheese.

Jackpot! It's fate! I should kill him, or at least chop his dick off and stuff it in his mouth.

I wondered if his severed testicles might fit into his eye sockets, if I popped his eyes out first, that is.

He crossed to the small fridge to fetch a beer. "Want one?" He asked. My head pounded as he spoke, a sudden flash of pain rippled. My senses heightened. I could smell sweat and pot. Despair and failure. Cheap cologne too.

The back of his nasty shirt was stuck to his back as if it had been shrink-wrapped on. In my mind, I pictured myself stabbing him.

Just do it and run. Leave this shitty place. Kill the fucker.

I planned the steps I would take, the fury I would feel. The power and the thrill that would belong to me alone. My hand grabbed the knife handle, excitement rose inside me…

***

Two hours later, I was sitting on the floor in his trailer, alone. I was staring into space at a grimy cupboard door. I had no memories. Nothing. It was as if my mind had switched off or powered down all by itself.

Shit! Where is he?! What happened? Did he escape? Another blackout?

Blood covered the cheap lino floor. I scrambled up and stared down at myself. I imagined Greg might be walking into the emergency rooms with stab wounds or telling police officers about the crazy women who had just tried to attack him in his trailer.

Fucker must have knocked me out! Shit!

I was furious with myself for letting a stupid, filthy man get the better of me.

I ran.

I raced back to Grace's trailer, she was still sleeping, passed out. I grabbed my bag, changed my bloody shirt, took her money and I was gone.

One bridge burned to a cinder.

Back at the bus station. I expected sirens and lawmen and women at any moment. Nothing happened. I sat and waited and ate burgers. The pain in my head vanished.

I'm having blackouts. I have a tumor. Shut up! Everything's fine! Stop worrying. No! I have a tumor. I'm going to die. No, I'm not. It's fine, it's all fine. Just blackouts. Just!

Instinctively, I headed for home, mostly because I had nowhere else I could go. Grace had been my first option. My only *kind of* friend.

I always had a hatred of people and their stupid ways. I tried to avoid everyone unless I thought they could be of use to me.

So, home it had to be. My very last bridge.

Home was a rickety, lucky to be still standing farmhouse in rural Alabama. I thought long enough to realize I was behaving like a wounded animal, trying to get back to its burrow or its nest.

I pushed the thought as far back as I could get it.

I tried not to think at all on the long journey home. My headaches returned on the second day of traveling and I popped pain pills like candy.

What's happening to me? Nothing, shut up.

I never used my cell phone much. I had no one to call after all, but I tried to google lumps people might find on the back of their head, then cysts and tumors. It all bored me, no image looked like mine. I tried to take a photograph of my lump, but it looked obscene, porn-like.

In the midst of silent passengers staring depressingly out of the windows and two particularly annoying children I wanted to throw off the bus, I fell asleep.

My cell phone ringing woke me, and I scrambled up to answer.

"Annie?" a male voice asked. I knew the voice, but hadn't been able to place it at first.

"Umm… Yes," I replied.

"Where are you? You were supposed to meet me at eleven yesterday."

It was my probation officer, I was due my weekly check-in, and I'd gone and forgotten all about it.

"Sorry, I'm not well. Upset stomach and it's very contagious," I lied. "Both ends you know."

"Are you at the same address?"

"Yes, I'm in bed," I added a groan for effect. In the distance, I heard loud noises and deep booming voices.

My stomach dropped and my senses heightened. I had a feeling I knew what was coming next.

"Annie, I'm outside your apartment. The police are here. Your boyfriend is now a missing person. Eric, where is he? It's a crime scene, they said. Blood everywhere. What have you…."

I ended the call.

Shit, I did do something to him! But where was the body? What the fuck is happening?

A vague thought spiraled in my mind until I caught it. I googled Grace's town.

There had been what they called a wild animal attack. In the trailer park. A shin bone was found, a single shin bone.

That must have been what happened then. An animal. It wasn't me. I just blacked out.

I am no fool. I did not believe my own thoughts. Still, it was a warm and comfortable lie.

I turned my phone off and took its sim card out. I crumpled it up and buried it in the dirt on our next roadside stop.

I used my stolen cash to buy plenty of food for the rest of the journey; I was ravenous. Back on the bus, I ate five pre-packaged sandwiches that tasted like Hell itself. Still, I was hungry. I ate one more. Three left.

The throbbing in my head steadily continued to worsen until it became blinding.

I hated headaches.

I tried to go back to sleep. I pictured myself lying on a beach somewhere, margarita in hand, food by my side. My stomach rumbled loudly while I dozed.

Brakes screeched and disturbed me.

I woke with a jolt, convinced the bus had been surrounded by police with big guns. Nothing, just another car overtaking. My stomach warped and spasmed. I was so hungry. I felt around for the rest of my sandwiches, desperate. Gone.

"Who stole my food?!" I stood up and yelled. "Which one of you stole it?!"

"Shhh," the passengers moaned. "No one moved."

"Calm down or you're off!" The driver shouted.

"Fuckers," I said and sat. God, I hated people. I wanted to kill them all.

I felt rage that someone had sneaked over and helped themselves to my goodies and left the empty packaging behind too.

They were mine, all mine. Silently, I fumed and watched the world go by. I plotted my revenge on humankind.

Pain started up at the back of my head. On my lump. It felt so sharp it made me gasp. I popped the last of my pills.

Roughly a hundred miles away from home, we stopped again for gas and bathroom breaks. I had my eye on someone from the bus, a lone male traveler. I was convinced *he* was the one who had stolen my food. It seemed the most logical conclusion. I watched him head around the back of a truck-stop diner. I followed.

"Hey," I said as I grabbed his arm. "Where are my sandwiches? Asshole."

He kicked at the dry dirt and sneered at me. I hated looks like that. He lit a cigarette and coolly assessed me.

"You callin' me a thief, girly? You ate them, I saw you." He had a slight grin on his face. As if he found me amusing. His words were lies. All lies.

That was it, it never did take much. Sparks of fury that were always present exploded. A red mist covered my vision. My limbs shook, my stomach flipped. Adrenalin and power surged inside me. Static filled my mind like a swarm. I stepped towards him… and then I found myself back on the moving bus.

What the fuck?

I scrambled up and looked around at the people. They all faced forward like good little passengers. Lone traveler man was absent.

Another blackout? What did I do?

Nothing made sense to me.

I felt fine. No bruises or scratches. No blood splatter on my clothing.

That must have been his stop, that's all. I shrugged, I didn't care. I felt brighter, no headache. I was okay, I was safe.

My whole body felt warm and strong.

I closed my eyes and took a seat in the wooden rocking chair in my mind. I tried to view the screen, to replay the memories I was missing. Tried to replay the events and what happened. Nothing but static was showing.

Close to home, my headache started up again. I decided to reach around the back of my head. I lifted my short hair so I could take a good feel around. I wanted to see if my strange lump had grown or sunk in some more.

Something razor-sharp sliced the top of my left index finger clean off in less than a second. I yelped in surprise. It didn't hurt, not one bit. Most of the passengers on the bus ignored me completely, although a couple tutted loudly at my yelp.

My finger was missing a large chunk, and I sat staring at it. I refused to believe what I was seeing.

Don't think about it, don't think about it.

I knew I couldn't run from the problem, not anymore, but the least I could do was go back to ignoring it. So that's what I did.

My headache eased very slightly. I wrapped my finger as best I could. I was only good at inflicting injuries, not healing them.

I leaned my head against the window, and I cried. Not actual tears, I've never been able to do that, but I made pitiful sorry for myself noises all the same.

It's important not to panic. Of course, I should panic! Shouldn't I? I'm going to die. I hate the world, but I want to live! Am I dying right now? How long do I have? Don't worry, everything is fine. I have a brain-eating disease, a parasite, a... I don't know.

I'm going to die. No, I'm not. Maybe I just need antibiotics?

We arrived at my drop-off destination while my mind argued with itself. I sought the nearest diner and ordered burgers and fries. Then I ordered more to take away.

I ate as I walked. I followed the familiar twisted rural paths home.

My mother was not at all happy to see me. In fact, her first words of my great homecoming were, "What have you done now, Annie?"

She stepped aside wearing an old flowery house dress as big as a circus tent, and I still only just fit through the doorway.

My brother Max and my younger sister Alice still lived at home. The rest of us had run as far away as we could get as soon as we were able.

I had no idea what half of them were up to or where they even lived. Besides, they all generally hated me.

"I just need a place to stay, Ma," I mumbled. "Please."

"You'll be needin' to pay," she told me. "I ain't feedin' you for free, girl."

I nodded and slipped past her. I expected nothing less. I was there for one reason only.

At the back of my mother's land stood woodland and an old cabin where we often played as kids. By play, I mean they did. I sat solemnly, left out, overlooked.

I had it in mind to hole up there. I explained my plan in short, clipped words and gave my mother three hundred dollars.

She immediately sent my dazed and permanently confused brother, Max, to the store in town. My mother loved her food, almost as much as I seemed to, but she loved money more. Her children were third on the list, I believe, or maybe fourth after the quiz shows she watched.

Even with all the junk she ate all day, every day. I doubted her good bear got more than the old table scrap.

I gathered up spare blankets and a few essentials. I paid another hundred for the privilege and waited aimlessly.

I sat at the table in the kitchen and held my pounding head in my hands. The pain had made me grimace, and I worried it might give me premature wrinkles.

"Y'all in trouble?" Alice asked, appearing from upstairs. I hadn't seen her for years and she was almost as big as our ma. Her hair hung in greasy childish pigtails and her bulbous breasts hung down saggy and low.

No bra? Really, Alice! For fucks sake!

She made my skin crawl on sight, but my stomach rumbled hungrily all the same.

"Trouble?" she asked again.

I shook my head.

"Runnin' from a bad man then?"

"Yes," I lied, nodded, and tried to remember how to look scared. My stomach spasmed and a little drool slipped down my chin. Quite suddenly, my disgusting sister looked absolutely delicious. My body jerked. I lost the battle for control of myself.

"Poor Miss," she soothed and came toward me, full-on fast speed for a big girl.

"Don't!" I tried to say and then I was gone.

The next thing I knew, I was sitting on the kitchen floor with a picked-clean bone clutched tightly in my hand. Blood gathered in a single large pattern and soaked straight into my clothes.

I panicked, stood up, and slipped back into the pool of blood face first.

"It's still warm," I whispered absurdly.

My mind couldn't fathom why I kept blacking out and then people vanished. Although, I admit a small part of me suspected. Okay, that was a lie. I kind of knew.

"Alice?" I said almost silently.

I wiped the blood from my eyes and looked around the floor, expecting to see her hiding someplace.

I could hear a quiz show playing loudly in the background while my mother shouted all the wrong answers at the screen. My ears buzzed and a moment of absolute terror and clarity hit me. I did it and I knew exactly how.

A brief, powerful thought swarmed in my mind, and I stopped it before it could play out in full. It wasn't the right time for thinking.

I didn't feel bad for Alice, not one bit. I felt bad for myself, my safehouse was ruined.

My mother chose the wrong moment to stomp heavily into the room.

"Alice, where's my… YOU!" She roared. "Killer! MUR-DERER!" She almost sang the last word and her voice trailed off like a failed opera singer.

I started to laugh. I couldn't help myself. The sound came out in great big snorts, and I belched loudly. A chunk of brain tissue flew out of my mouth and hit the wall where it stuck.

"Ha!" I said.

My mountainous Ma stopped just short of the blood pool, her face quickly turned pale as each of her chins wobbled. She remind-ed me of something, and the image of a turkey popped into my head, which in turn reminded me of Thanksgiving. Of course, that got me feeling hungry all over again.

She tottered and wobbled around slowly as if to get ready to run, and I laughed even harder at the thought of that.

"Guess which bear I fed Ma! Guess which!"

I laughed until my vision turned black.

Next thing I know, yep you guessed it. My mother was gone and so was my headache, almost.

Still, I was hungry. Famished. I pulled a single strip of torn clothing out of my hair. A piece of my Ma's house dress.

I sat back down to wait.

I heard my ma's truck, followed by Max's footsteps. He came into the house carrying several large brown paper bags.

"Back, Ma," he shouted, shutting the door with his foot.

"Ma," he yelled again. "I got us a bargain at that there store, I did."

He walked into the kitchen, goofy teeth first, and I smiled. It was fun to watch his expression change from joy to shock to terror as he took in the carnage and the scene.

"Come on," I whispered to myself. "Keep me awake this time."

And it did, I saw what happened. I knew what I became, and I liked it. Finally, I was me, a whole, complete version of me.

I was glorious.

I left the house eventually. I showered, burned my clothes, and put on fresh ones.

I took all the money I could find and a thick pair of gardening gloves. There were no valuables anywhere that I could find. I took my brother's plaid shirts and Alice owned a pretty patchwork quilt, so I stole that too.

I kicked over furniture and I ransacked drawers and cupboards. I did everything I could to make it look as if the scene was a robbery gone wrong and I enjoyed doing it. I'm no expert, I don't know if I made the scene believable, I only ever saw a few episodes of CSI.

I didn't know what would happen, with no literal bodies to be found. But sooner or later, someone was bound to come looking, and they'd fetch the sheriff. There was still the small matter of all that blood and pieces of bone too. Not to mention the few teeth I spat out.

So of course, I ran.

I took all the food I could carry, and I made my way to the long-forgotten cabin.

It was clear straight away that the place had been abandoned years before. I almost didn't find it, thick walls of bushes and trees made it half-hidden from me.

For the first time in a long time, I smiled a genuine smile.

***

It's not so bad here. It's damp and it's cold at night, but it's safe. A night ago, red and blue lights lit up the night sky. I assume it was the sheriff up at the house. That's okay, really it is. No one will find me here. Maybe my family will get their own Netflix crime special someday. I might be the star.

Oh, and there is a mouth on the back of my head.

An actual, honest to God, living, mouth. One lined with multiple layers of sharp vicious teeth.

Thanks to the thick gardening gloves, I even know it has a tongue.

An impossibility. A physical and literal, very anatomically impossible thing.

But yet it's there, it exists and it's extremely hungry. How does what it eats even get into my stomach? I'll be damned if I know.

The headaches are back. When they get too much, I tell it that I'll shave all my hair off so it can't hide.

Or I threaten to go to the dentist. It doesn't like that, and the headaches fade a little.

In the silence, I can think. I am not a good person and I never have been.

I killed a man once, for pushing my temper too far and I enjoyed it, such a lot.

He was beautiful to look at too and I buried his body far too shallow. I drank vodka while I dug his grave, drank and drank.

He was found two weeks later but the killer was not. Although a young woman was caught drunk driving close by, the same night he vanished.

He was not the first person I killed either. My sister, the one who fell from the window, wouldn't have fallen if I hadn't pushed her. I enjoyed that too. You wouldn't believe how annoying she was. And, there were others, including my cellmate. I favored surprise attacks for killing. Shock and awe tactics. I am underestimated.

My mother was right about me.

Being good takes the kind of energy I wasn't born with.

Many people in this world are like me. None of those grow a second mouth. So, I think and I think, and then I think some more.

I have a few theories as to why I came to be this way.

It could be possession of some kind, just like in the movies. But I never dabbled in the occult, it always seemed like too much hard work.

It could be a very rare disease? I found mention of such a thing in Japanese folklore. Futakuchi-Onna she was called, the two-mouthed woman. Maybe I'm just like her? If something exists in one culture, why not in others?

I wonder if my true inner self became conjured up on the surface. That this affliction somehow came from within me, from inside me.

We expect the terrors in our midst to come strolling out of sewers carrying red balloons or crawling out of old wells with a horrifying face draped in long black hair.

The real monsters are your own friendly neighbors, the lover who shares your bed, or the mean woman on the long-distance bus. They are your family and friends, the people you love, or the ones you like to be around.

You don't expect a person you might know to be a killer. One with a sudden and insatiable appetite.

Or the likeliest cause, the one that fits the most. My new mouth might be the result of a curse or hex, one sent by the family of the dead man I killed. Maybe a spell that was meant to force me to speak up and confess went awry.

Perhaps they didn't count on the murderer being someone like me.

You see, I never minded killing in the first place and I've never been the squeamish type.

It's these damn headaches I can't stand.

Luckily, I know a good way to stop them. I'm hungry. I'm ravenous and in these parts, it's almost hunting season...

WOMEN OF FIRE AND VINE

Part One: The Void

Layer after layer. Flesh of intricately designed twisted atoms formed on unnatural skin. Membranes. A secret level, a dimension connected yet still separate. Everything yet nothing at all. Born of darkness and of light, a hidden realm existing between the two.

A land divine refuses to tread, a realm where evil itself became lost and afraid. Sin, conflict, wrath. Fury invoked, summoned, conjured with glee.

A special place, with a purpose to serve, to change structure, mass. Energy fashioned, manipulated with cold grace.

Created by rage and feminine anguish. The first scorned woman created above and below in reverse.

A space between spaces. A world within and without.

A new hidden realm, one seeped through cracks unseen.

A place for after. For the chosen few, selected by thresholds of pain, intolerable cruelty.

Bloodshed formed the ground; betrayal formed the skies. Murder, vile abuse, formed the rot inside. Despair and anguish created the realm in between. A slip through the borders. A world of the lost and never found.

Strict order, freedom, chaos, absolution. No redemption inside the Void. A dark reflection in an ornate, pretty gilded mirror. No heaven. No hell. An alternate.

Not belonging to infinite, but to the other. Indifferent strength. Sins are collected, provide fuel. Vats of suffering. Harmony missing.

Energy cannot be destroyed in the Void, instead, it changes. A chrysalis anew.

God looked away. Closed His most righteous eyes. The Void grew. No abyss, it was never emptiness, to begin with.

Powered by vengeance. A place for the female, the sacred wronged women to be reborn. Transformation. Metamorphosis. Rebirth. Revenge.

Opportunity.

The First, Fire.
1693

Catherine stands shivering, bound, even as the heat fast approaches. Thick rope, fastened with complicated knots keeps her tied firmly to a wooden post. She cannot move.

She already tried to run and failed.

She was caught, and swiftly too. Her innocent body was probed for Devil marks, searched. Invaded by the brutal coarse hands of hysterical, manic men caught in religious fever. Clothes were ripped from her body. She was beaten, held down, forced. Spat upon, cursed. Viewed as a damned body by the diseased false righteous minds of men and nothing more.

She is innocent of all crimes accused. Vile accusations. None heard her cries or protests. None listened to her pleas, her desperation. None pitied her tears. No trial. No hope. Only punishment of death by fire.

A child went missing, taken by wild animals. Catherine knows this, she saw it happen, too quickly. Herself helpless against the wild, hungry beasts of the forest. Yet still, they blamed her. In hushed whispers, pointed fingers, and narrowed eyes, they plotted. Accused her.

Her, Catherine, with her questions of God and her wild, untamed ways. Damned for walking barefoot in the woods and enjoying the cool light of the moon. They blamed her for the loss of the fair-haired child, claimed she sacrificed him to her red-skinned, horned God, the fallen one.

Flames lick closer, the burning, stinging heat.

She screams and jerks, the pain already too much to bear. She coughs wildly, smoke fills her young lungs. She searches the crowd through thick black smoke as blisters form on her delicate skin. Pale flesh quickly turns to red glistening sores. Layer by layer, melting away.

Her family, she sees them. Two parents, one little brother. They watch her burn with greedy eyes.

"Mother," she coughs into the scorching heat. "Father, please."

The pain. White-hot agony. For a moment, consciousness is lost. Her mind is cruel, it keeps her aware. She jerks her head and screams as the orange flames lick her bare legs, eating away.

She can smell meat cooking. Her own self cooking alive.

She cries, afraid and betrayed by the whole village of thirty devout settlers. Her body is the evidence of their wrongdoing, their sins, and now it will turn to ash.

Let me die, let me die. Please.

Catherine does not call out to a bitter fallen angel, a biblical God, or his resurrected Son. She does not believe in any. A secret she will take to her grave, one she didn't dare to speak. She believes in the magic of nature, the old ways some still whisper about.

Help me, help me, help me.

Her heart still beats as she suffers. Madness caused by brutal agony takes hold. She welcomes it, anything to escape the pain.

She screams once more; the wail holds promises. Secrets, it swears revenge on all.

"Burn the Witch, Burn the Witch," the crowd chants. They are excited, aroused, some even gleeful. One man laughs, the leader of their settlement, the man of the church.

He enjoys the sight the most. "Burn," he whispers.

Catherine does burn. Blood, bone, flesh, and tears. She burns until she is no more than black soot and ash.

***

Under the layers in the realm of the Void, hot lava bubbles and flows. The nerve and muscle beneath the fleshy surface part. Lava twists, gathers, shapes, and fashions.

Something new grows and forms. A she that holds the energy of a thousand scorned, and betrayed women is born. A smokeless human shape of fire and flames.

Spiraling energy, held together by forces unknown. No atoms, but something new. She has texture, structure, encased together, molded into a female shape.

She holds one desire, one goal in her new existence. One absolute aim. Birthed by her own death.

Reprisal, retribution, revenge. Pure malevolence and something more contained inside. Intolerable anger rages in chaos absolute.

The figure moves, driven by vengeance. She roars into the black sky above her. Sparks shower.

She will seek and she will find.

Whispering voices circle her, hushed talismans, guides to help. They speak a language of emotion only she can know.

Sparks of ember fall from her shape as she walks. Ash trails behind her.

A coherent thought flashes, a place she longs to be. Memories tumble in a whirl of madness. She remembers. She was Catherine. Was. She was scorned, burned, betrayed.

Sparks fly as she screams. Flames that were once her enemy dance by her side as she seeks obliteration.

A doorway opens, a hole, a breach leading to a chance, a prospect.

Whispering voices, the sounds of a thousand scorned women encourage, inspire, and provoke her.

She moves. An exit. The whispers follow.

She finds herself in the place she lived before. In the world she inhabited before her renewal.

A pang of familiarity causes her a sudden jerk. A cluster of houses, a white wooden church, a village. The beginnings of a new town. The site of her betrayals. The settlers. A bitter scorched circle in the center of their brave new, stolen land. The evidence of her ending remains. A word flashes, her whispers speak.

Patriarchal.

She knows the word but cannot recall its meaning. Still, she hisses as she stands. A shower of sparks lands close by. The night is a thick dark black. It does not prevent sight. Not for her.

Quickly and with ease, she travels. Walks as fire in her world from before.

She calls the whispers, insists on action. Yearns for it. Flames kiss the ground and spiral around her. Focus, clarity, begin to seep in.

She sees a house, one made of plain wood. A flicker, a wave. Flames separate and hungrily attack the timber. Each flame spreads, eats, and consumes with passion, eager to please their mistress of wrath.

She repeats the motion. Two houses burning. Startled, terrified screams begin.

The leader, the vile imposter in the house of God is her aim.

The cruel man inside. The twisted man, the accuser of innocence, the defiler of women.

She knows inherently that she will not be dominated. Not be beaten. Never again.

She is destruction in a burning force.

In the blink of a human eye, she moves and stands ready, gazing at God's house.

Somewhere close, frantic voices. A single bell begins to chime.

She recalls she used to like the sound, but now it is her call to war.

Two men run towards her, rifles in hand. They freeze as they see her. Her glorious form of fire and fury.

"Satan!" one shouts. "It's the devil!"

Not Satan. No Devil. No fallen, winged, pretty feathered angel.

Instead, the wrath of woman. A far deadlier force.

Flames shoot from her arms and hit the men. Their clothing bursts into flames and their cries of agony only fuel the ravenous fire as it scorches them alive.

The church door swings open, a man stands. The ringleader, the accuser. The arrogant, cruel, treacherous, fool.

She sees him.

The woman made of fire roars. Spits heat. Slivers of orange, red, and white fall from her. None can be extinguished. All catch and spread, wild and free.

The man flails in shock and falls. Down the few steps to land at her fiery feet in terror. A second roar. She hurls a white-hot flame between his legs. His suffering is her victory, her win, her conquest. She watches as he writhes in brutal pain. His manhood, the thing that fooled him into false superiority, burns black. Charred remains of ash.

Inside him, his organs heat rapidly and pop. His heart thuds and struggles. His cries of absolute fright and pain are her delight.

She claps once and laughs wildly. Sparks drift into the air.

The dying leader knows who she is, recognizes or senses. He knows, even though his mind is aflame as he burns.

Behind her, thick bellows and screeches sound. The villagers all run back and forth, each one disturbed by her invasion, all frightened.

For her, they are her targets, she wants them all to burn. Needs it, craves it.

A man and a woman dart by, a boy dragged by their hands. She sees them, recalls them. Her former family.

Flames flicker and dart like arrows. Heat bites and licks. Eats them alive as they shriek in terror.

Skin blisters, melts away. Still, the flames want more. Greedy and hungry.

Buildings fall, crackle, and collapse. A flurry of ember rushes into the sky. The church is aflame, smoke thickens the night. The cross that once stood proudly at the top falls and crashes to the ground.

Ash rains down. Whispers chatter and laugh with glee.

If God sees he cannot intervene or will not.

Bodies fall to the dirt tracks. Suffocated by smoke, melted faces like wax seals. All dead. All suffered. All felt the fear and terror as she did.

Cries of fear and agony fade. The small community is no more.

The whispers cluster and circle their mistress. Somewhere, under the layers of flames, she smiles.

She is power, force, revenge. She will dominate. She is without mercy. A gift, sent from the Void.

Part Two: Vine

NOW

The woman sits tucked into a cobwebbed-covered corner; her head hunched down low. She does not know where she is or who she is, only that she *is*.

Her mind has faulted, withdrawn hastily, hidden away. Images flash before her eyes, pictures she cannot touch, feel or taste. She senses only one emotion, one single twisting feeling spiraling around inside her as it tries to find an anchor, a place to settle and latch on tightly. Fear, in its purest, most primal form.

Besides her, spiteful thistles, as thick as rope, grow and weave in tangled knots. Angry, razor-sharp thorns as large as herself threaten to pierce her. A bleak grey sky hangs over her head while clouds of fire hurtle above her. Surrounding her is darkness, sheer blackness impenetrable to her vision.

She senses evil, wickedness.

Vaguely, her mind conjures a rhyme. No, wait, a prayer. A half-forgotten verse meant to bring comfort. A flicker of memory from childhood, a sliver of spark from the past.

She tests her mouth, tries to speak.

Her voice echoes, her uttered words muffled, "I shall fear no evil, for thou…"

The rest is forgotten. No, a shimmer of thought, a flare of recall. The woman tries again, "For thou art with… me."

Encouraged, she speaks her prayer aloud again, she finds velvet rhythm and smooth cadence in the sounds. "Though I walk through the valley of the…" She stops.

A scuttling sound alerts her. Something unseen listens to her desperate words. An absence of life lingers close. Watches and waits.

The woman squeezes her eyes shut in fright. She wraps her arms around herself and cries out loudly. Her movements are a replay of an event from before. Her actions jerk a memory loose, free.

A barrier inside herself comes tumbling down, a dam breaks, floods. A torrent of brutal terror engulfs her.

A vision flashes across her mind, a movie playing all by itself in her jumbled mind.

A group, a group of friends, family, shadows. Her, on the edges. Just her. Alone.

An empty pit inside herself. A weak connection severed in two. Betrayals, one by one falling like dominoes. A cascade of abandonment.

She took a way out, a brutal ending, an exit just for her. Realization hits, the harshest of blows. Despair follows quickly behind.

"I'm dead," she whispers. "I'm dead… Is this… Is this Hell?"

No redemption. No finish. No obliteration after all.

Thoughts collide with devastation. An explosion inside herself. She tries to climb to her feet. Tries to do something, do anything. Thick angry vines writhing like serpents grow and appear. Each one wraps itself around her legs. Traps her, imprisons. They squeeze, pull, tear, and slice.

She screams in horror, terror, confusion.

"Please…" She cries. "Please no."

Around her, whispers. Furious whispers rise in a mocking crescendo. A thousand eyes and yet none at all watch her struggle. The glow of light above her chooses to leave. All light exits.

"Help," the woman screams.

There is no one to help her. No one to hear her. No one willing at least.

Wait, a glow of amber light. A single flame of hypnotic fire.

Closer it comes, closer, closer.

An inferno, a burning inferno in the shape of a woman. A blaze of hair trails out behind her. Embers fall. A firestorm of hate.

She approaches, slowly, gliding. Turns her burning head and narrows glowing eyes.

Assessing, considering, deciding, accepting.

In a blink, the woman of fire vanishes. The ground quakes in solidarity.

The woman screams again and feels the loss of heat.

A forceful yank pulls her down, more black vines grow, twist, and reach for her. Each one grips tightly, pulls. A cold enemy embrace.

Her vision swims and she sees. The whispers speak a fury of secrets, instructions.

She knows. The woman understands. Comprehends.

She gazes at the tall black grass, an anti-nature, an abhorrent land beneath her feet.

An afterlife, all after, but no life, a reverse of being. A mocking existence.

Animation of despair. No Hell, but a crack, a gap. A space between spaces. A Void, endless in its fathoms and depth. The women of fire, the leader of the strange in-between land.

"Thou art with me," she gasps as she begins to sink.

No. She realizes God is not with her. God is absent.

There is something else present entirely. The woman of fire appears once more. It is her world.

Light extinguished, hope drained away, never welcome in the Void.

The flaming force beyond her comprehension watches with curious indifference, absolute in superiority.

Heat shimmers as she approaches, leans in close. Minds swap, ideas, information. An exchange, a deal. A pact. She understands. Stops resisting.

Vines scratch at her eyes and ears, press, and explore. She welcomes the intrusion.

A sharp jab as one enters her skull, in through her temple, forcing, growing, overcoming. More vines penetrate, pierce skin and bone. She does not bleed nor feel pain, her heart fails to beat.

Vines of parasites overcome her, invaders. She is not afraid.

The woman is pulled down, down, endlessly down. Swallowed. The whispers follow, excited, curious, hungry.

THEN

Anna gazed out of her window and wondered if she had become invisible. She held up a slender hand and tested to see if she could peer through it. She could not.

I'm still here, she thought. I can see me.

She pinched her skin, just to be extra sure while she waited for her therapist to call. Her weekly session had been rearranged into a ten-minute phone conversation and her therapist was late to call.

She's forgotten I exist. I know it. Just like everyone else.

Anna swallowed mild despair. The medication she took daily helped her keep a handle on her feelings, a binding cage around her emotions. She had come to depend on the daily doses of numbness that slid down her throat so easily, so greedily.

Anna felt alone in the world, deeply, truly, utterly alone.

Anna was not wrong.

When Anna was born, her mother discarded her, refused to embrace her, denied her love.

From her beginning, she was cursed to be unwanted, a fate she couldn't change.

Her foster mother left her abandoned and forgotten outside a supermarket entrance, crying unheard. Then later, left her hungry and sobbing while she lay passed out from heavy drinking. The trend continued into an everlasting pattern of parental neglect.

Siblings were born and fostered. Those were cared for, fussed over, admired, and wanted. Anna stood gloomily in the distance, overlooked, and unseen. Lost.

Her birthdays were spent entirely on her lonesome or surrounded by a raggedy circle of silent, old stuffed toys.

In her school years, Anna was ignored. She found she wasn't clever enough to join the groups of geeks and nerds, not pretty enough to join the popular girls. Not sporty enough, not fun enough. Just plain and average. Entirely unnoticed. No friends, no comfort, no hope. Barely acknowledged.

In college, she flew under the radar too. If she were ever brave enough to speak up in class to ask a question, her teacher would frown, unsure. He'd stare, blink rapidly, and say, "Sorry, your name has slipped my mind. Who are you?"

After the third time of him doing so, Anna stopped asking questions, stopped attending college. No one noticed.

People, strangers, would knock into her. None would apologize, almost as if they couldn't see her at all.

If ever she spoke, nobody recalled her words. As if they couldn't hear her. As if she were nothing more than an annoying mosquito buzzing around, an irritant, and no more.

In her circle of friends, she lingered on the edges, a shadow. Never part of their shining group, never one of them. Still, Anna would try to call.

"It's who? Oh, it's your birthday? Oh, I forgot. I have no time. We have families now. We all have children except you. We're too busy."

Busy yes, together, without Anna.

Social media photos showed them all out in a happy group. A smiling bunch, enjoying drinks and a meal. No invitation for Anna. No thought of her.

Anna craved love, to be adored. Eyes never landed on her, hands never touched, no romantic smiles, no hope.

At work, Anna had a small desk crammed into a room with large desks full of vibrant happy people. Coffees would be made, none for her. Sandwiches would be fetched, none for Anna. Overlooked, unseen, forgotten.

Sometimes, her own boss would act surprised to find her sitting at her own desk, he would act confused. Anna had worked there for five years before she overheard him ask who she was for the fourth time.

Anna withdrew further from a society that never even acknowledged she existed. She longed for her place in the world and failed to find it.

Anna attended a Church, she sat at the back as if she were a mourner, mourning for her own lost, neglected self. She cried tears and stared blankly, recited a prayer for comfort, one half-remembered from her childhood.

"For thou art with me…" She stopped, mid-sentence. Defiant. "No… you're not. No, you're not with me! Nobody is," she spat.

Anger surged. She stood and kicked the pew, a spiral of rage raced through her. She ran. No one stopped her, no one saw her desperation.

Anna ran into a coffee shop, fueled by the need to be around people and noise. She stood in a line, a long stretching queue. No eyes landed on her, no one asked her order. The server skipped by her entirely, utterly unseen.

She ran into the street; rain pounded the slippery pavement. Anna fell. No one helped, no one stopped. People walked around her, irritated by her presence, bleeding alone on the ground.

"Can you see me?" She yelled to a stranger. "Am I even here?" The stranger chose to avoid her.

Ignored, she stumbled back to her lonesome flat, neglected by all. Heartbroken.

On her thirty-first birthday, Anna thought over her life. She stared down from her window seat in her tiny second-floor flat, as people rushed by. Happy people, talking together, holding hands, smiling, and laughing.

None saw her, none looked. She had received no cards, no messages, no acknowledgment.

What if I just blink out of existence? Or sink into the ground and become no more? Is that what happens when you're forgotten?

Tears slipped from her eyes, slowly at first until her body shook with great big sobs.

The pain inside her grew. Agony twisted and spiraled out of control. She wanted to scream, yearned to wail, and race around the streets shouting.

Would anyone see me then? Nobody ever sees me and if they do, they want someone else. I'm never good enough, never.

She wiped her face and looked at her phone. No messages, no calls. In a burst of bravery and defiance, she called her therapist's office.

"Hello, Nicola didn't call me. It's urgent. I'm… really… I'm struggling."

"I'm sorry, she must have forgotten. I'll have her call you back straight away," the receptionist informed her. The phone call ended before she could speak again.

I'll be okay, she'll ring me. She'll help me.

Anna waited, no one called. Minutes turned into hours, still, no one called.

"Why?" She screamed. "WHY?"

She paced her small room, while rage collected in her stomach. She yanked at her hair, pinched her skin, just so she could feel anything other than her turmoil. She had no one to help her, not a soul, and she knew it. She put on every light, still, the rooms felt too dark. Always too dark.

Emotions overflowed, feelings of hatred and bitterness swamped her. She caught a glimpse of her reflection in her mirror. Fury engulfed her, she picked up a lamp and launched it at the shiny surface. Shards of glass showered down in a violent rush of noise. She pounded her fists against the walls, frantic with the need to be heard and seen. She wailed in internal agony. Tired of battling against a wave of loneliness forever attempting to drown her. She screamed, a primal scream of deep, twisted pain. A plea for help.

No one came. No one noticed.

"I'm real," she sobbed. "I'm here, I am!"

With desperation, she called her sister. Call rejected. She called her foster mother, Louise.

"Mother," she cried. "I'm not doing too well. Can we talk? Help me, please."

"Yes, well, neither am I. I've no time sorry. My legs hurt and my hips are bad. You know I have problems; I can't deal with your silly drama too." The phone call ended.

She called her brother, Peter.

"It's me," she said.

"Who?"

"Anna."

"Anna, who?"

"Your sister! Peter, please, I need to talk to some…"

"Sorry, I'm very busy."

Peter ended the phone call. There was no one else she could call.

She threw her phone far away from her, a shard of pain pierced her heart.

This is all too pointless. I'm no one. No one and nothing.

Anna once had dreams. She dreamed of being an actress on Broadway, a singer in a theater. Her voice was beautiful, rare, perfect, and no one even knew, no one ever stopped to listen to her sing.

Anna once believed in God. She sought comfort in prayer, sought God in her loneliness. Instead, angels turned their backs, turned to stone under her crisis.

I'm nothing. I don't want to be here. I don't want this anymore. I don't want to exist.

"I can't any longer," she told herself. "This is torture."

Anna reached for a knife, one with shiny life-ending, promising edges. She wrapped her arms around herself and wailed. She cut her wrists; the pain only fueled her further. Blood pooled, collected around her. She laid her head against the wall and cried steadily. She wrapped her arms around herself and waited.

No more, I can't stand it. Not anymore.

She yearned for the release, for her body to die, for everything to end. Her most desperate finale to end her suffering.

Her life drained away, onto the cool hard floor. Her broken heart failed, stopped entirely.

Anna died as she lived. Alone, and betrayed. Neglected.

It was three weeks and two days before the people downstairs complained about the smell and the sudden appearance of flies. Twenty-four days before anyone noticed, before anyone found her. Longer before anyone cared she was even dead.

NOW

Down, down, lower, lower.

Rage seeps in and fashions anew. Marrow turns vile, bitter, angry. Skin hisses, shivers, quickens, rots. A transformation, one of flesh and energy. An easily beaten battle of wills, no contest.

The woman does not resist, cannot. She welcomes the change, she craves it.

A vicious scream of anger and fury leaves her darkened mouth. Vines, tangled black vines, with razor-sharp edges, an abhorrence of nature, exist inside of her and flourish.

Something saw her living struggle, something terrible acknowledged her pain and existence.

She was noticed, chosen. The woman, Anna, embraces the bleak in all its twisted, wicked glory.

She joins with the Void. Submits, welcomes.

Its corruption spreads, sin, and immorality become part of her. Its wickedness becomes her flesh, its evil, her mind.

Changes occur.

Coherence shatters, illusion falls. The ground vibrates with birth pangs. Tremors form. A second scream rages, a primal scream. One full of fury. Brimming with revenge.

The ground parts, Vines pull back, their job finished. Rotting arms find places to grasp. New strength powers the flesh-covered body. Substance is given, borrowed, and loaned.

The woman is birthed. Not fully Anna, not anymore. She is something new. The malicious land fashions darkness itself.

The emotion of vengeance grows. Whispers encourage her, help in her birth. The woman of fire watches her. She steps back.

A final scream, one of triumph. Anna laughs, the sound is brittle dry leaves crushed under feet.

The sky groans and cracks apart, a breach, a door. A way out. Not an escape, but an opportunity. A chance for revenge.

The Void sets her loose. The Void sets her free, and watches.

Anna's therapist, Nicola, sits in front of her television, a glass of wine in her hand. Her eyes stray away from her huge expensive screen as she shops online for shoes she will never wear. She stops to fill her glass. She is thinking of a hot bubble bath and nothing more when she hears the sound.

'Scratch, scratch, scratch.'

"Toby?" She assumes. Toby is her cat. Blessed with senses keener than hers, he has already chosen to run.

'Scratch, scratch, scratch.'

Nicola stands and groans, intent on letting Toby in or out. Instead, she freezes and squints. A shadow. It enters her home, drifts through the wall, and stands still in the corner of her living room. A grey translucent figure wrapped in rope. No, not rope, sharp gnarled and tangled vines. The sounds of whispering fill her ears. The figure flickers.

Nicola rubs her eyes and focuses.

"What the…!" She gasps. Her wine glass falls to the carpet. She jolts and drops to her knees in shock.

Her bladder gives out as the figure steps forward. Transparency gives way to solid.

Nicola can smell rot and decay as the figure forms the depth and texture of a woman.

"Please," she begs in disbelief. Her mind refuses to accept what her eyes tell her. Instinct urges her to run, still, she cannot move or stand as the woman bears down on her.

With a single brutal movement, the woman of vines grasps her firmly by her throat. She is captured, damned. No escape.

"See me," new Anna hisses like a serpent. "Do you see me now?"

Nicola realizes she knows exactly who it is, feels the knowledge. Her mind swarms with the guilt she failed to feel upon hearing of Anna's death weeks before.

Her mind plays an image, a scene of Anna waiting for her phone call, waiting to be helped but ignored instead. Nicola feels a rush of pain, a wave of neglect. She feels the loneliness and despair Anna had. She is being shown.

"I'm… I'm sorry," Nicola babbles. Too late. Useless words. Pitiful apologies.

Her body quakes and shudders as she begs. A skeletal hand reaches out for her face, fingers of bone decorated with thorns probe without remorse.

The thing that was Anna is swift, it jabs sharply. A popping sound fills the room, a burst, a squelch. Nicola screams in terror and pain.

The woman holds a single torn-out eyeball high as if she has won a trophy. Ripped nerves dangle freely. Nicola tries to stand, tries to run.

The skeletal hand holds her firmly in place. Blood pours down her face. Her own hands fly up in her defense.

"Please," She wails. "Please."

The woman of vines has no mercy, no compassion. She lacks both entirely, reborn without.

A tendril of twisted vine escapes her form, sharp with jagged edges. It wraps around the throat of Nicola and squeezes.

Nicola thrashes wildly, dying. No air, no breath. Agony fills her mind as she dies slowly, yearning for breath as Anna herself had once yearned for. Anna relishes her suffering, feeds from it, enjoys it. Craves more.

Nicola's body is discarded, left twitching on the plush carpet.

Anna remembers everything in one crushing blow. She flickers as emotion and abandonment threaten to overwhelm her. She knows who she was, knows what she is. Understands what she has become, comprehends what changed her.

She sees the dead body, feels no guilt. She only seeks more in her hunger for vengeance. Whispers surround her like fluttering birds, encourage her in their excitement.

She leaves.

Anna's brother Peter sits clipping his toenails on the edge of his bed. He tries to catch the shards as they fly, dreading the complaints of his wife if she ever finds a stray one.

A sudden breeze catches him off guard. Briefly, he glances at the window, certain it's locked.

He shrugs, absorbed in his task.

'Scratch, scratch, scratch.'

Again, he looks around. The room is dim, and he is alone. Home all alone.

'Scratch, scratch, scratch.'

"What is that?" He mutters. Annoyed, he gets up, crosses to the window, and pulls back the long heavy curtains. He staggers back quickly.

"Wh…" Is all he manages to say.

He falls to the floor in shock. Incomprehension.

A grey figure taps at the window. Scratches it with a single long brutally sharp thorn-like nail.

Within seconds it folds impossibly and drifts through the thick glass, through a tiny opening, and into the room. As its mottled feet hit the carpet it becomes more solid. A she. Rotten flesh and sinew form before him, substance grows. Thick vines wrap around its human shape. Matted hair trails down its back. Dark amber eyes peer intently at him, studying.

Peter's mouth hangs open, eyes wide. He sees. He knows. He feels. The noise of whispers fills his mind, like a hive of bees.

"Brother," she says.

Peter shrieks a high-pitched sound as the vine woman races towards him. A skeletal hand plunges into his chest, muscle and nerve burst apart.

White-hot agony fills his mind and body as Anna finds her goal and yanks. Gleefully, she holds her gruesome prize. Peter watches as his own heart beats in her hand once, twice, stop.

"Do you see me now?"

Peter cannot answer. Blood fills his mouth as he gasps, gurgles, whimpers, and dies.

The woman laughs a deep low cackle. Power fills her, desire increases.

She is everything she ever longed to be. She is seen.

Anna's foster mother Louise sits watching her nightly soap operas. She is absorbed by the plot, taken in completely, unaware of her surroundings.

The figure enters her home, under a small gap, an unnoticed crack. Louise does not see. In the dim light of the room, the figure gains solidity. She approaches, a smile on her moss-covered face. The television set bursts with static and shuts down.

"NO!" Louise shouts. "Not now!"

She sits in a reclining chair, feet up, resting. She moves to pick up her phone, to call someone for help. Finally, she stops and hears.

'Scratch, scratch, scratch.'

She cranes her head behind her, sees thick sharp vines with deep thorns drag along her carpet like tentacles. Before she can speak, or cry out, a hand grips the top of her head, a fierce grasp, full of violent, impossible strength.

"Neglect," a harsh voice speaks into her ear. Whispers fill the room and laugh.

A second hand shoots out, one covered in rotten black moss. Impossibly strong boney fingers travel over her face to probe her lower jaw.

Louise begins to spasm, a heart attack. Before her own body can fail her, her lower jaw is yanked down. Muscle and cartilage pop, bones snap. Blood pours. The figure twists her head in one easy motion and rips. Severed, discarded, thrown away, abandoned. The head comes to a rest in front of the television, wide dead eyes watch the blank screen.

The woman leaves. Still hungry, still vengeful, still wrath.

The thing that was Anna walks down a street. She does not know where she is, only that she *is*. Memories play in a slideshow across her mind's equivalent. She watches each one without emotion. She wanders, tirelessly. Anger swirls inside her, a focus of fury. She wants to obliterate, needs it.

All pain is forgotten, her abandonment is beyond recall.

She feels one thing. The desire for revenge.

For her, select people shine like beacons. She cannot leave until the lights of her enemies, the ones who failed her former self, and others like her, are extinguished.

She longs for her own new world, the Void. The place where madness is welcomed, and pain is admired. A space between spaces. A gap between worlds for the carefully selected.

She seeks only to destroy, anguish trails behind. Wrath of karma. Her vines scratch surfaces as she passes, chills anyone close. Moss and rot fall away unseen.

No one can see her. Now that is her advantage.

Some can hear her whispers, her company, her talismans. A hive mind of a thousand voices of lost women, the feminine abused and betrayed. Anna is their vengeance, their new voice.

Only the marked, the chosen, the beacons will sense and see. She searches and finds. She craves to be seen by them. *Will* be seen.

A force of delirious revenge. A cacophony of misery and violence. She found life in her death. In her cathedral of chaos within the Void of the fire woman.

Hunger stirs. She desires, she needs, she finds. A beacon close by. A light to smother. She smiles and seeks her way inside.

MAIDEN, MOTHER, CRONE

I heard them before I caught sight of them.

Voices, the male human kind. Low and gruff, an earthy noise. I stretched, unsure and uncertain. For a moment, disorientated. My senses picked up a new sound: the scrape of rocks, the obnoxious hammering of unpleasant iron, deep laughter.

How long has it been? Who woke me? Why are they down here?

I knew my slumber must have lasted many years, decades even. I could feel changes, deep in the layers of my private self. I could sense a difference in the earth too. Poison and distress, a cry for help. Balances shifted. No harmony above. Sacred lands and special sites leveled, taken away, and destroyed. Only our ancient circles, our doorways set aside.

Has my kind been forgotten?

Another sound. Footsteps, heavy feet scraping on rough rock. Each step edged closer.

Quickly, I moved. I watched with interest, curious, unafraid. Darkness was never my nemesis.

I hid in the cracks, up high on the rock face, peered down over the edge into the chasm.

It was supposed to be my secret sanctuary, a place I could sleep, to grasp the changes of the world in peace. A chamber I could thrash out my inner turmoil. A slice of the world that was something of my own. One where humans would never dare to tread, a forbidden realm to them, deep underground, my subterranean land.

Voices inched closer. With narrowed eyes I saw, watched.

Three men. Each one with bright lights resembling a sun for a third eye. They walked in a single line, carefully, as if they expected the jagged stone layers to collapse underneath them. None wore armor, none carried swords, none had a purity of heart. None had grace in their heart. Loyalty was of no value to them.

Only one had hair on his face, the rest were smooth like a child. Each carried a turtle shell on their backs. Spider webs of rope linked and joined them as one.

What madness is this?! How long have I been sleeping? How much have I aged?

As a Maiden, I was wild and free, the ultimate trickster, a teaser. Stories were told about me around a fire in the night, ballads were sung. Males tried to catch me and steal me away. I enjoyed beating them at their own egocentric game. For centuries I played. I was nymph and consort, oracle and queen, a prophetess with an eye on the future.

Maenads envied me. Pan himself took a bow in my superior presence.

I was adored in my cathedral of forest. Worshipped by my congregation of nature. Desired, the huntress I was.

My mother phase was altogether different. I refused to submit whenever I choose to step into the human world.

We each know the stories: a man catches a beautiful, other-worldly woman, he tricks her, removes her ability to shift back into her true form, and hides her magical skin. He forces her into becoming his wife, his bedmate, cook, cleaner, and insists she have his children, and so on.

Lies.

A story invented from a man's desire to overcome the female and nothing more. Seal women were captured, yes, tormented, bound to one realm. Revenge was always theirs, an escape back into their own world. A plummet back into the oceans, their former husbands dead or insane, punished without redemption while the seal woman laughed with glee from her place within the waves.

As a Mother, I chose a human husband. Me. I charmed each one. I chose the pure of heart, the passionate, the provider. None caught me. I was the one doing the catching. Great Kings and knights, nobles and peasants. Poor men or rich. Mine. I snatched at will. Devoured or loved. Slaughtered or treasured.

There were many who succumbed.

It is in our Crone phase when changes occur. Some of my race fade into obscurity, some become the bitter villainesses of fairy tales and folklore. Some become an unrivaled force, a wanderer, primal energy itself. Some return to Gia, or back into our true Fae world. A few cease to exist, they disappear into obscurity. Our monthly blood stops draining away. Some feel their life and power fail too. Three phases of the moon and three of a woman.

I chose to sleep. To wait. To dream until the shift inside me completed. To wait and see what or who I would become.

Until they woke me.

I heard them talk as I scuttled my way across the damp rock face. I followed. They spoke and planned on spending the night to dream, deep in the private confines of Earth. Breathe in pure air that was mine to enjoy. Each one felt excited, I could feel the anticipation, those brave explorers. All of them overjoyed to be mapping out a new unexplored cave system.

My system.

Anger inside me began to spiral. Hunger caused primal desire. Emotions ran amuck. Fury twisted. My hands gripped ancient stone and crushed. The rock, the powder, the remnants of my rage, fell in a loud shower.

The men ceased talking. Each aimed their third eye sun at me. I roared in fury. Seen. Savage hunger. I was ravenous.

I dropped.

At their level, in a small chamber, I crouched. They towered above me. I stood in my sure magnificence. I swiped and clawed, absorbed and repelled. Feasted on shock and horror.

The first fell. I slashed his throat before he even knew he was down. Blood gushed and caused delirium inside me. The second, I pinned against the sharp, jagged wall. My unrivaled eyes met his. He feared me, and deliciously so. He begged, pleaded. My hands, weapons of sharp, harsh nails, tore into his slimy clothing, into his skin. Nerve and sinew parted; bone snapped easily under my rage. I yanked his beating heart out. Once, twice it thudded in my grip. I bit deeply, swallowed, replenished.

Still, I craved more.

The third man froze and whimpered. Hot, salty tears slid down his face. I licked each away and soothed him. He sobbed for his fallen friends; I admired his brief compassion.

"Sit," I told him. He collapsed in a tangled heap on the cold, rocky ground. A shaken, weak man, afraid and cowering. "Tell me about the world above," I demanded. "Tell me everything."

I learned a great many things as he spoke. I listened carefully to each word. He talked of wonderful new terrors. Iron birds flying in the skies, snakes of metal traveling the land. Electricity and technology. Earth, dying, poisoned by human ways. Species extinct.

He spoke until his voice faded entirely. No longer useful, I pulled him apart, explored inside. No changes had occurred inside a human.

I ate his liver, feasted on his heart. Satiated temporarily. I snapped his neck, languished in his terror and pitiful cries for his mother.

It seemed I had been asleep for many centuries. I had missed so much, too much. In my attempt to hide from my natural rhythm and cycle, I had failed myself as well.

There was a new world above. A polluted, disease-ridden, war-raging, cruel world. Gone were the knights of old, gone were the ancient ways, the old ways. My ways.

Some men no longer had honor, no longer had pureness of heart.

Only greed lived inside the many. A new age had dawned. One of narcissism. The worship of self.

A new system was in place, one still run by pitiful, egocentric men. However, women were rising, some had searched inside and realized their strengths. They were fighting back, overpowering, and succeeding. The wilful, feminine divine was awakening. The power a woman holds is great.

The female could not be defeated. Still.

With new fresh desire and longing, I searched through the backpacks of the men, not turtle shells at all. I found clothing ugly but necessary. The third eye was not a sun, but a torch. One I didn't need in order to see.

I raced up to the surface into a brave new world, to find a brave new me. I emerged from the cave system, a new force.

Earth had cycles that matched my own. I understood. The earth would be renewed and now so was I.

The Crone holds power like no other, power in experience, transition, memories. A strong will and body, no weakness. All resilience.

I ran to find water. I drank deeply and admired my reflection. I was still beautiful; I had always been beautiful, and now others would see the regal in me. Others would adore me and fall down on their knees to worship.

Who would have thought I would find new life in what I believed was the beginning of my ending? It was never my finale, after all.

I languished by the water and stretched. Animals moved and clustered close, eager to see their newly emerged leader.

My senses picked up the scent of humans nearby. Hunters. Not hunting for food, but for fun.

Not so different after all.

Eager for the chase, I stood, I roared. I ran towards it.

It is my land, and I am Queen.

A ROSE IN THE WINDOW

Ever since we bought the house in the countryside, I haven't been able to settle.

At first, it was only that I couldn't sleep. Instead, I lie awake for hours staring at the twisted cracks growing strong in the ceiling, only to fall into a slumber so deep I have nightmares I can never recall. I wake up full of terror so brutal I lie breathless for hours.

Then I forget all about it. Why do I forget?

I remember that the strange word turophobia means the fear of cheese, but I cannot recall where my most favorite lace dress might be.

I like flowers, roses, and tulips. But what did I eat today?

Sunlight shines and I blink. When I look again, the moon has replaced the yellow brightness.

I cannot settle.

I feel as if the house doesn't belong to me. It doesn't feel real or substantial anymore, if it ever did, to begin with. We signed the lease, or rather, he did, and the home became ours. It was supposed to be a new beginning, an adventure together, one just for us.

Why does he never speak to me anymore?

I hate this house.

The spiraling staircase is dusty. I wipe and scrub with no effect. I wonder how I even got here, how my life came to be landed on this destination, in this house.

I want many things in my life; I want to travel and see glorious sights. I want to stand in open outdoor markets and smile as people bustle by. I want to see my friends, my family. I want to swim in an ocean and watch the waves crash on the shore.

I cannot settle.

All I do is wander and wait, and I don't even know what I'm waiting for.

I think I knew once, a half-forgotten memory sometimes stirs within, but before I can snatch and examine it, it's gone, trailed away to sit along with the dust that never moves when I wipe it.

I found a bottle of perfume. It isn't mine.

Is it?

There is a smart new washing machine and tumble dryer, still shiny and new. I remember the day it arrived, how he grunted and yelled, trying to make it fit in the small gap put aside for such a thing. I laughed at the absurdity, the comedy of the angry scene. I can't work it. Even now, it is as much as a mystery to me as this home, this house.

I can't find a mirror. I did once, but it fooled me. The mirror was a trick, the glass inside fake somehow. One of his cruel jokes, I expect.

Sometimes, the house fills with the smell of freshly cooked bread. The scent fills my nostrils and my mouth waters in anticipation.

I don't remember baking it; I don't remember eating it. But I must have, I suppose. He ate it, I heard him say how delicious it was and I smiled, relieved he liked it, relieved I did one thing right at least.

This house makes no sense, I don't know where I am most days.

I get lost in the labyrinth of hallways and pretty ornate rooms. One sunny morning, I was in the bedroom, the main one with the good mahogany furniture. Before I knew it, darkness had fallen, and I heard him laugh. That deep chuckle of his, the one I used to love. A wave of dread engulfed me, a shatter sensation pierced me deep in my heart.

I'm always cold. Is that why I can't settle?

I asked him to turn on the heat once, the rambling old heating system the estate agent promised us still worked. He ignored me.

He does that now and no matter how many times I ask him, he won't turn out the lights at night. It's too bright, it blinds me. He won't listen.

I fear the house. It is my enemy.

Sometimes I cry in desperation, but tears won't seem to fall.

At first, the house was my friend's and I loved it. I liked to wander in the vast garden best of all and plan which flowers I might grow, which special ones to plant and encourage into bloom.

Roses, I decided. Pretty red roses, with blood-colored petals, ones I could enjoy on those balmy hot summer nights I liked the most. I picture an image of one red rose standing in my delicate glass vase in the window. I want it to act as a lure. A lure of what delights may lay beyond in our wonderful garden.

I even dug a place. I ordered roses, a spade, and some compost. I made a home for my pretty flowers. I had everything ready, and I think that's where he put my body.

I hardly felt the blow to the back of my head. When I did, it was too late. My memories slipped away, along with my life.

He never spoke a word as he killed me. Not one word.

There is a new woman here, she won't leave. I shout and I beg, but still, she ignores me and stays.

This house frightens me. I wander and I forget. Yesterday, or weeks ago, I screamed at them both. He told her he loved her. Words he never said to me with meaning. They pretended not to hear me. I lashed out. Kicked the antique coffee table, the one he insisted on buying with my money. It was always my money we used.

The cups, my pretty China cups, rattled from the impact. They both left the room, horrified, briefly. They made jokes about me as if I wasn't there.

I cannot settle.

I'm always cold.

I found my favorite lace dress.

It's hanging in the wardrobe along with other clothes I don't recognize. Did I buy them? Are they mine? I hate them. Short dresses and low-cut tops. On my dressing table, a brush with long brown hair tangled in it. My hair is blonde. Have I dyed it?

I can't find a mirror that works.

I cannot settle.

I gaze out of a window. The woman is out there, in my garden. Tending to roses that were meant to be mine. Blood-red roses. The same color that ran down my face as I fell from the impact. My body must feed them. My roses are part of me. Yet here I am.

Is she the gardener? I forget. I suppose she must be.

What did I ever do? I think I hate this house. I don't want to be here.

It's far too cold.

He comes up the stairs, the twisted banister held tightly in his grip. I scream. He ignores me.

I tell him I cannot settle. Still, he pretends I don't exist. Pretends I'm not in his way.

Anger stirs, confusion overwhelms me. He was always so mean, so callous, so cruel.

I push him.

He falls. Over and over, down flights of stairs. The ones I always hated climbing.

He shrieks and wails. I don't like the sound.

I peer at him. At the face I used to love. His eyes are open but still, I don't think he sees me. He soon turns cold while my roses are pruned outside. The gardener, if that's who she is, is doing a good job.

It's cold. I hate this house.

At least now I can settle.

FATHER DEAREST

Perspective, I like that word. Sometimes I roll the letters around my tongue so I can enjoy the feel of it. Perspective can sum up a hundred different views, all of the very same events.

The deep and dark horror movie style pit on the edge of our land, for example. A disused relic and dangerous hole to some, the home of slithering monsters to my younger siblings.

For me, it's the resting place of my father. Although, he isn't actually resting.

He went tumbling down the pit, bouncing off the edges and screaming his wretched sounds of fury and despair. All the way down into that bottomless hole until finally I heard the faint thud as he landed. Followed by the wonderful sound of blissful silence.

I was the only witness to his accident, which was very lucky indeed.

You see, I'm the one that pushed him.

I often think that people are capable of impossible things. You hear the stories of a frantic parent suddenly able to lift a whole car after an accident to fearlessly rescue a small, trapped child.

Amazing feats of strength, powered by pure love, under the right set of adrenaline-fuelled circumstances.

I think it's possible that the same power might work in reverse. A good person can become suddenly capable of what others might call a horrific and sudden act of evil.

For as far back as I can remember, I always hated my father.

While other fathers would delight at their child's first steps, mine would wait for the inevitable crash to the floor so he could sit around laughing, beer and bible in hand.

A meanness lived inside him, desperate cruelty grew, and in him, it flourished.

There was no love in his misshapen heart of hatred that I ever witnessed. My father liked to blame his own children for the state of his life, for his home, and for the state of his own terrible self.

A vile man, by all accounts.

I was born first, the eldest by a year. I was named Ruth. My mother died during childbirth. She bled to death giving birth to Nellie, my youngest sister.

Mother gave birth to six of us in total. Two died as soon as they were born, but not one single tear was ever shed by our father.

Life was tough before she passed. After Mother's death, the four of us surviving children left were raised in filth.

He hated us. Father despised everyone.

Mother was the rock that bound us together. She could control Father, just enough. She kept his anger at bay, made him keep his fists and harsh leather belt to himself.

Without her, our lives fell apart.

Grime soon covered every visible surface; carpets became torn and dirty. Furniture sat broken, the old sofa had a hole big enough to swallow you up into its spring and foam-filled abyss.

The windows were cracked and held together by thick black electrical tape, and two panes were missing entirely. Cupboard doors swung loose or were long gone. As soon as I was deemed old enough, cleaning became my job. An impossible task.

Father would sit in the only good chair we had, reading his bible over and over. He would pause to shout out particular quotations and bark out orders while he ate bag after bag of sweets, drank beer after beer.

When he wasn't eating, you could hear him mumbling, scratching, and picking at his own skin.

Pick, scratch, pick. Mumble, mumble.

He started off picking at his nails until all that remained were bloody stubs. Then he started on his fingertips until he advanced to his whole hands and arms.

Chunks would be missing like tiny bite marks; little pieces of skin fell to the floor like confetti. Sometimes, he bandaged the worst bits, but mostly he carried on.

Pick, scratch, pick, mumble, until his hands resembled a severe burn victim. That still didn't stop him.

He was troubled and mean before Mother died. Her death caused his anger to simmer to a boil and erupt.

Sometimes he climbed into our old car to visit the shops, coming back loaded with brown paper bags full of sweets and beer for himself. None for any of us.

We had a kind of stepmother for a few months. A pleasant lady who met Father in church. He could put on a charming act when it suited him.

He played the part of a sad, lonely widower well.

She ran for the hills as soon as Father got drunk and lost his temper late one night. She left so fast that she forgot her handbag and her car. I doubted it was the hills she ended up in.

"And he shall rule over thee! Genesis, 3:16," he bellowed at her the night she vanished for those mythical hills.

Father did love his bible passages. He had one for every situation.

The poor woman hadn't been a permanent fixture anyway. We all knew she wouldn't stay or be told what to do. I liked her.

After that, Father got drunk every night.

He took to being surprised when we were around. He said things like, "Why aren't you damn feral kids in school?" or "I thought there were only three of you?"

My little brother Tom became his favorite, and by that I mean he got fewer beatings than the rest of us and he always had an extra serving of food, whenever we actually had any.

Tom was good at quoting the bible. He paid attention, and he learned fast.

Father would ask me to repeat his favorite passages. I never would.

"You don't listen!" He raged. "You have the Devil in you, you spiteful, evil child!"

He liked to remove his belt and beat the demons out of me. He said I was full of sin and corruption.

"In the beginning, God created the heavens and the earth. Genesis 1:1."

When he started with that sentence, we had to listen for hours and hours.

My sisters were too young to really understand. And me? I believed that if God existed, he would have killed my father Himself.

We had no other relatives that we knew of, no one ever came out to visit. We were a forgotten, isolated family on the very edge of an overlooked and failed, half-derelict town.

The land was bad, all barren. Nothing would grow. Even weeds refused to flourish, except for the hardiest stinging type or the poisonous nasty kind.

When I had just turned fourteen, I took to sitting on the splintered window seat in the room I shared with my sisters. I liked to gaze at the stars and think, but worry always got the better of me. I worried that if I ran away, my siblings would suffer more in my absence. I worried that if I stayed, I might never be able to escape.

I knew there was a world out beyond my reach, a whole beautiful world to see and experience, and I yearned to be a part of it.

I knew it couldn't all be misery, cleaning, hunger, and bible lessons.

Pick, scratch, pick came the sound from downstairs. *Mumble, mumble,* as Father drunkenly moved around.

As my sisters slept, I started forming the beginnings of a plan deep in the depths of my mind. The thing that really triggered my desire for his death was the way he'd started looking at my sister, my eight-year-old sister. I had to act.

The next day, I woke up early to pointlessly clean the windows. I had a perfect view of our barren garden. The old pit. It sat at the end of our property and had long ago been covered with weak metal sheeting.

No one knew who built it, and no one seemed to know why it was created in the first place. I recall asking my mother once. She'd only shrugged and told me it had always just been there.

It was a hole in the ground. Three meters wide and pitch-black inside.

We were forbidden to go near it.

I snuck outside, lifted the metal sheet, and I heard sounds from inside the pit, a kind of tired gurgling, almost like the noises our stomachs made. I assumed it must be old water, still trickling from the nearby overgrown pond. It smelt of rot and decay, sulfur and moss.

I knew Father sometimes dropped beer bottles down. I suspected the nice lady from church might be down there too.

I dropped a small rock down and waited. I counted the seconds until it hit the bottom. Eight glorious seconds. I guessed it was deep enough for someone to go plummeting to their death. At the very least, a person would be trapped inside and die eventually.

Getting Father outside would be the hard part.

I tried and failed for four days. Father wasn't the type to fall for trickery. He only chose to move if there were something in it for him.

A year before, I fell down the stairs, arms full of laundry I had to finish within an hour. I busted my ankle pretty bad, and I screamed. But rather than help me, I got a slap around the head for disturbing his reading.

"No," I yelled. "Get off me."

Instinctively I pushed him away from me.

"Whoever curses his father or mother shall be put to death," he shouted. "Exodus 21:17."

He tipped the dirty washing over me, kicked me, and dropped the basket on my head for good measure.

I had to get him outside.

I felt as if I had nothing to lose. Truly.

I walked into the living room and told him Tom had fallen down the pit. My voice shook with fear, but that only added to my believability.

"We were playing. He slipped and I can't pull him up," I said. "I'm not strong enough like you. I can see him. Clinging to the edge. Tom's falling Father."

I saw a range of emotions play across his face before he predictably settled his expression on anger.

He came barreling at me, quicker than I expected for such a large man. A shower of sweet wrappers and flakes of skin fell to the filthy carpet.

"I'll kill you, Devil girl, you just wait," he spat. "Thou shalt not suffer a witch to live. Exodus 22:18."

He hit me hard.

Hard enough so that my ears buzzed, and I fell against the wall. He stormed out, thundering across the front lawn while I battled to get my senses back in time.

I had a kind of tunnel vision at that moment, perfect clarity and focus. All I could see was his massive behind as he peeked down into the pit.

"Tom," he shouted. "Are you down there?"

He was just working himself up for a second yell as I swung and hit him in the back of his head with our chicken shit-covered spade.

"You!" He spun and gasped, wobbled. Blood poured down the side of his head as his cold eyes turned full of the purest hate. I became filled with the certainty that it was either me or him in those precious seconds.

So, I pushed him.

I gave him one big old mighty shove and off he went, down, down, down. Bouncing off the sides and screaming all the way.

I heard the thud as he landed, the snap of some essential bone.

I threw the spade in along with old straw and newspapers. Old rags and soil too until I felt confident he was covered up if anyone happened to stop by and peer down. I replaced the metal sheet and held it down with more old bricks.

I walked steadily back to the house as if nothing had happened. I cleaned myself up and gathered his precious sweets into a pile.

I shared it equally between the three children as I explained that Father had grown tired of us and left.

"He's run to the hills," I told them.

Children are more resilient than you might think. There were a few tears of confusion, but the treats did a good job and dulled the upset just fine.

"Things will be different now," I told their beautiful, dirty faces. "Very different."

The next couple of days were challenging. My siblings were overwhelmed by their new sense of freedom. They were no longer confined to their rooms but running free like children do and should.

I made a fire outside and hoped no one from town would bother to come looking for its source. I burnt old furniture, rugs, and Father's clothes. I bathed my sisters and watched the dirty water drain away, hoping our misery would go along with it, swirling away and off down the drain.

Tom took his own bath in privacy, bribed into the water with promises of more sweets.

On the third day, I cooked, cleaned, and took stock. I found a large pile of money hidden in a dresser and that made me very happy.

In the evening I was sitting in the one good chair so that I could think and make clear plans when I first heard it.

Pick, scratch, pick, mumble, mumble.

My veins turned to ice as I waited. The sound felt as if it came from the house itself, from inside the walls and under the ground.

Pick, scratch, pick, scratch, pick.

I paused to wonder if the noise came from my own guilt-ridden mind. I shook my head rapidly as if to send the thoughts away.

I paced the room and held my ground, raised by the father we all had, had made me fear almost nothing. The more I heard the sound, the more I became full to the brim with anger until it toppled over.

"You will not ruin our lives anymore," I seethed out loud.

The sound stopped abruptly but I was spooked all the same. I took hold of our one flashlight, and I went out to place extra bricks on top of the metal sheeting which had slipped off.

I sat and stared at the pit. I wondered until morning came.

The next day presented problems. We needed food. I couldn't legally drive the old car, but that didn't worry me. I didn't want to leave my siblings and I couldn't take them all with me.

Forced into a corner, I told Tom he had to be the adult, be the man of the house while I went out. He puffed up his chest and took to the role just fine, so I made the drive into town feeling pleased I looked older than my years.

I expected to be questioned, and I practiced my answers on the way. But no one bothered me. I filled the cart with good and decent food. The shop clerk raised a penciled eyebrow at me while I tried to smile sweetly, but nothing more.

I got home and sat a moment, gathering my breath before I put everything away in its proper place.

Pick, scratch, pick, mumble, pick, pick.

I ran into the living room, furious. I found absolutely no one. On the floor, by his chair, on the ground I cleaned and scrubbed repeatedly, sat pieces of freshly picked skin.

That night I put my siblings to bed, freshly washed and with brushed hair and teeth.

I sat in the living room, and I waited. I almost fell asleep, and then I heard it.

A slow shuffle coming towards the house, my house. I stood quickly and headed to the curtains to peer out.

They say love never dies, but maybe hate doesn't either.

I watched as my father stumbled across the dead brown grass, almost naked but with bits of his trousers hanging off him in strips. His huge stomach jerked and wobbled as he lurched.

Black and green slime covered him nearly head to toe as bits dropped off and trailed behind. His mouth hung wide open. His eyes were nothing but white staring orbs. His left leg bent backward, stuck at an odd angle, and he dragged it uselessly, using the spade as support.

His face stayed locked in a grimace of rage and despair. He was dead set on our front door.

He was coming for me; I knew it. I hadn't killed him properly and now he wanted revenge.

Wild panic ignited inside me.

Pick, scratch, pick came the sound as I clamped my hands over my ears. My heartbeat drummed relentlessly in my ears.

The shuffling came closer, and I darted to the kitchen for the biggest knife I could find, fully prepared to kill him again.

"Mine now," I raged. "This house is mine. The children are mine."

I yanked open the door and ran into the empty night to find nothing. No one was there at all.

It's all in my mind. Guilt? My imagination? I told myself. Do I expect God to punish me because I killed him when he should have?

I hadn't felt a single ounce of guilt when I pushed him, only freedom. But I suspected that maybe I felt it somewhere inside me anyway and I just didn't know it yet.

The next day, I started to teach my sisters how to read. We joked and laughed; we drank fresh fruit juices, and ate warm baked cookies. Tom discovered a tin of paint in the old shed out back and he hummed away, happily painting the hallway. He did a very good job too, and I hugged him proudly.

For the very first time, he didn't flinch.

In the evening, I lugged the television upstairs. We ate popcorn and cuddled up under a blanket while we watched the Wizard of Oz. It was my mother's favorite, and we hadn't been allowed to watch it because Father said the Devil made it.

We all enjoyed it. I knew we each had more courage and heart than any of the characters.

All of us fell asleep in a tangle like newly born little kittens.

I woke to the sound of shuffling outside and the familiar noise. *Pick, scratch, pick, mumble, mumble.*

I held on tight to my family and tried to only think of good thoughts.

The sound wouldn't quit. I stayed quiet until it hurt my mind.

The scratching started up on the front door.

I crept down.

Pick, scratch, pick.

I didn't open the door. I leaned against it and I prayed. I pleaded with God to help me.

"Vengeance. He will bathe His feet in the blood of the wicked. Psalm 58:10," I heard my father hiss.

"Go to Hell," I answered. "An eye for a fucking eye. Exodus 21:24. Bitch."

I dragged a heavy chair across and barricaded the door. I sat on the bottom step and waited until morning.

The next day, I concentrated on my siblings. We planted seedlings in freshly dug ground.

In the evening, I bathed my sisters and put them in bed. Both of them hugged me hard.

I sat on the stairs with the biggest knife we had, and I waited.

The shuffling started at around midnight. My father stood at the closed front door. I listened for breathing, but he didn't take a single breath that I could hear.

"This is my house now," I told him through the door, and I swear I heard him growl in return.

Pick, pick, pick. Scratch, scratch, scratch.

"I'm not scared of you," I whispered. I repeated it over and over until I believed it myself.

We stayed at a stalemate on each side of the door.

"An eye for an eye," he said, just before the sun came up.

I heard him shuffle away as dawn arrived. When I finally opened the front door, there were no tracks. But a small pile of freshly picked skin lay settled on the doorstep.

I knew I faced a choice. I could either give in to the fear, my own hidden guilt and paranoia. Or I could try to undo the damage he'd done to all of us, me included. Hate is a heavy burden to carry. It leaks into the deepest part of you until it eats you away with its bitter poison until there's nothing left.

My mother always said something was wrong with the land we lived on. She said nothing could grow or thrive. But thinking of all the hate Father had inside, I knew something could grow. It all depended on your perspective.

While my brother and sisters tucked into a fried breakfast, I poured old petrol down the pit.

I set fire to a cleaning rag and threw it down with a flourish.

The bang I hadn't expected shook the house, and it knocked me clean off my feet.

I landed on the grass with a thump, scooting backward, then spinning and racing up.

My family stood at the door with open mouths and wide, fearful eyes.

I couldn't help myself, I started laughing. A deep, manic snorting laugh.

Soon, it was all of us doubled over giggling.

"Ruth. My tummy hurts," Tom said. He wasn't used to laughing. He stood with a precious strip of bacon clutched in his hand, happy tears streaming down his face, and that started us laughing all over again.

"What went bang?" My sister asked.

"Father did," I told her. "Father went boom."

***

Years have passed now and since that day, Father hasn't come back much.

I don't know if it was the fire that almost finished him off or if he really did die the first time around. But I do know one fact: things can grow on this land after all. Things can grow plenty, and they can thrive.

Father was evil, cruel, twisted up inside and the land reacted. Or maybe it was the other way around.

My siblings and I took that vicious hate and we overcame it. We pulled up every bad weed and destroyed everything mean on our land. Every time something nasty grew back, we pulled it out again until it gave up its fight entirely.

We grew pretty flowers and good food. We talked about Mother and never mentioned him.

We banished all the hate, and we replaced it with love every chance we got, and so love started to grow and thrive. Pure love.

Sometimes, when I wake up in the night, I can hear him.

Pick, pick, scratch, pick, mumble, mumble.

On occasion, I find dead, rotting bits of picked flesh on our doorstep. But that hasn't happened for a long time now. I think his power has faded some.

I plan on filling the pit in soon and pouring concrete down the whole drop, just in case.

I don't view myself as a murderer. I killed one to save four. I defeated evil and I have no regrets. After his death, we were happy. We were loved by each other. We were safe, healthy, and well. We were free and bad memories faded from the land and from inside us.

And Father was wrong, I did listen. But there was only ever one bible passage I liked.

Hatred stirs up strife. Love covers all offenses. Proverbs 10:12.

SIGNS

I knew he loved me within the first few seconds of our meeting. There was this particular *look* in his eye. He fell in love with what he saw; he wanted me, and why not?

I worked hard on my new image, especially for the job interview. I choose my outfit with great care. I spent over an hour straightening my long, freshly colored hair. I even watched YouTube videos and learned how to apply contouring techniques to my face. I looked different. I looked good, I felt good. I wanted the job as his receptionist, I needed it. Even before I met him.

"Please take a seat," he told me. He gave me that *look* again.

He saw in me a magnetic quality. Thunderstruck, lovestruck. His world changed when his eyes met mine. I knew it.

While a deep level of understanding settled between us. We began our charade.

He made a show of going through my CV, my list of office skills, even though I knew he must have read it twice or more already. He twisted his gold wedding ring around his finger and peered at me. I imagined the ring suddenly felt like an anchor to him, a bound chain he wanted to lose.

I swept my hair back and waited. So many emotions hung unspoken between us.

He tapped his pen twice and cleared his throat.

"You understand," he said. "That on some nights, I need to work late. Meaning, you might have to stay too? Everyone does at times. Is that a problem?"

That was code. I knew exactly what he *really* meant. I could feel his intention hang in the space between us.

He was handsome, clever too. After all, he had his own law business. I read between the lines and answered his loaded question.

"Of course, I'm more than happy to stay behind and… help."

For a second he glanced at me and frowned, narrowed his pretty eyes.

Have I read this wrong? Again? I thought. No, it's real, I know it.

I held my breath as my stomach dropped to the plush carpet of his office.

"Great. Can you start Monday?" He asked.

There! That look again! That glint in his eye. I recognized it. I'd seen it before in other men, after all.

Yes! I'm right this time. I know it, I just know it.

"Of course I can," I smiled.

"Then you're hired. Welcome to the team, Miss. Cleeve."

"Please, call me Lucy," I said.

He stood and shook my hand. His strong one fit into my delicate hand like two puzzle pieces destined to be connected. He held it for a second too long and I felt certain then. Absolutely certain. A burst of electricity passed through him and spread across my skin.

He was making two deals with me, although only one was official. The other would be our little secret.

That was all it took. Our first meeting. The start of our great love.

I told my probation officer that I would be starting work. "That's great," she said. "Congratulations. I'm pleased you're doing well now."

She wanted to know all about the where, the who, and the what.

I wanted to tell her the truth: that my boss, Micheal, had already fallen in love with me. I knew that because of the looks, the way he twisted his ring, the way he smiled and looked into my eyes.

More than female intuition. We had a bond. Of course, I didn't tell her anything. I knew she wouldn't understand.

People like her, with her solid marriage and her collection of children, had no idea of what life is like when no one loves you. Lonely doesn't begin to cover it. I wanted love, real love. I needed it so badly, and finally I'd found it with Micheal.

All weekend I dreamed of what it would be like between us. I imagined we might take long walks in the park together or stay in bed late on Sundays. We could have movie nights and fancy dinner parties. I would be a gracious host, elegant and beautiful. I would make him proud, I wouldn't be alone anymore. Never again. Inspired, I poured my medication away, they went down the drain along with my sadness. I didn't need them anymore. I was loved, I had hope, I had a future.

On Monday morning, I woke up early, happy to escape my tiny flat and become part of the world once more. I dressed in a pencil skirt and plain white blouse. Nothing too showy or attention-drawing. I guessed our love was going to stay a secret, just for me and him to enjoy, at least for a while. The other staff shouldn't know, couldn't know.

I arrived at my new job early, eager. A kind older woman took the time to show me around, show me how things worked and what my responsibilities would be.

We were finished after lunch. I sat at my new desk, waiting. Every few moments, I would see my boss and soon-to-be lover pacing his office.

I decided I would buy pretty underwear with my first paycheck. I gazed at him and wondered which type he might like the best.

Which color? Blue? Pink, white? Maybe black?

"Miss. Cleve," he summoned me to his office. "Can you take notes for me and type them up?"

"Of course," I answered.

He spoke wildly while I scrambled to keep track. I searched for a code in his words, a way for him to tell me how he felt and what he wanted from me. Instead, it was all law and office jargon. I nodded my head and crossed my long legs. His attention slipped to me, and he paused, eyes drawn to my limbs. I always had nice legs.

"I think that's it. If you could type it all up?"

He was flustered. I could tell. The skin on his face turned red, I could practically see the steam rise. A small drop of sweat slipped down his face.

"Anything else?" I suggested in my most luring voice.

"Not today, thank you."

That's code! That must mean tomorrow! Yes! I knew it!

I left his office and went back to my desk. The shrill phone beside me rang. A woman, asking to be put through to Micheal, her husband.

"I'm sorry. He's busy," I lied. "Very busy." I put the phone down on her.

I didn't like her voice, her tone. She spoke to me as if I were no one.

He has to leave her now. Or she has to leave. I won't be a mistress, not with a special love like ours.

At the end of the working day, I watched him leave. He winked at me on his way out and swung his briefcase once.

That's a sign. Our code! It has to be! But what does it mean?

I scrambled up and followed him out. He held the elevator, just for me. I slipped in beside him.

"So, how are you getting on?" He asked.

The door opened and other people were crammed in with us, so I knew he had to be careful what he said.

"Just fine, thank you," I grinned.

A woman sneezed and jolted. Micheal took one step towards me. I felt my pulse quicken and my skin hiss.

He's going to whisper something.

"Micheal," a deep voice said. "Can I have a ride? My cars back in the garage, more problems!"

My heart sank. Our chance was lost.

"Yeah," he answered. "No problem."

He looked sad, a little lost. I wanted to say something, anything to make him feel better. The elevator stopped at the car park level, and I lost him in the rush.

I went home, back to my grimy flat, and gazed out at the traffic below me. I wondered if he was thinking of me and if his wife suspected he was in love. That night, I couldn't sleep. The walls closed in, sounds were too loud. Every time I closed my eyes, all I saw was him.

The next day, I started early.

I wanted to make a good impression. I made a big pot of coffee and arranged a bag of chocolate donuts on his desk. I licked each one as I placed them on a plate and settled in at my desk.

"Morning," he said as soon as he walked in. He strode into his office, and I smiled. He popped his head back out.

"Are those treats for me?!"

"Yes, enjoy them," I answered.

He was thrilled, I could tell. I knew it. His eyes had that glint, he gave me that *look* again.

The day passed slowly. I answered the phone and put everyone through, except his wife. I finished all my typing, all my duties.

At five in the afternoon, he came strolling out and swung his briefcase four times.

Think quick! What does that code mean? It's a sign. Should I follow him? Is that it? It has to be. Go quickly! Maybe he's going to tell his wife he met someone else?

I shoved all the paperwork I had in front of me into a drawer, shrugged my thick coat on, and ran down the fire escape stairs. I wasn't going to risk the elevator again.

Right at the bottom, on the car park level, I hid behind a wide weight-bearing post. Just in time. He stepped out of the elevator alone.

Do I go and talk to him now? What if someone comes?

His car was all black, an expensive one with leather seats. I gazed as he unlocked it with a beep and glanced behind him.

He's looking for me, this is a test or a game! It must be.

As soon as he climbed in, I darted to my own worn-out car and followed him out into the night.

I was careful to stay exactly two cars behind him. I wasn't sure what his test might be, or what I should do, but I know I needed to pass it. At some traffic lights, I indicated to go left while he signaled right.

Shit! Concentrate!

From behind, someone beeped at me. I raised a middle finger in return.

I carried on following Micheal along twisted city streets until we drove into what I thought of as a wealthy area. Huge houses stood in elegant rows, all with their own double garages and neat gardens. His home was the biggest. He parked on the drive. I pulled over a few houses down and killed my lights.

Now what do I do? What does he want me to do? Do I wait here?

I watched him walk inside, into the warm amber glow of the house. He swung his briefcase three times and scratched his head.

He wants me to see. Get closer, he wants me to.

I felt out of place in such a rich area, still, I climbed from my car and walked casually along the street and up his drive. I tried to stick to the shadows as much as I could.

A single tree sat soldier-like near his main window. I raced across the lawn and hid behind it.

My view was perfect.

He knows I'm out here. Should I let him know for certain? No, he knows. Just watch.

Micheal was sitting at an old wooden table, an antique table with six high-backed beautiful chairs. He had his laptop open while a tall, harsh-looking woman with blonde hair in a complicated knot handed him a drink in a pretty glass. The wife.

Her mouth was moving, she was talking and using her hands to describe something. She was dressed in an expensive outfit. Smart trousers and a beige shirt. Effortlessly cool and beautiful. She laid a hand on his shoulder, a hand that should have been mine.

Micheal himself looked bored, distracted, sad. In his hand sat a silver pen. He clicked it twice.

His mouth moved, he spoke briefly. The wife smiled and left the room. He held his head in his hands for a second and rubbed his temples firmly. He knocked back his drink in one go, clicked his pen two more times.

He's unhappy. He doesn't want to be with her. Is this what he wanted me to see? It isn't a test, he needs me to see this.

I stared at him. At the slight grey strands in his hair, the beginnings of wrinkles around his eyes, his posture, his expression. He stood and poured himself another drink, knocked it straight back, and poured another.

He drinks so much because he hates his wife? Why can't he just leave her then? What am I missing?

It was then when I realized. The pieces fell into place. There was only one conclusion. He wanted me to witness his life, to see his relationship, to view his sadness. To really see, not just look. That meant one thing.

He wants me to kill her.

I crept away and drove home to think. Sometimes, people confused me. I knew that, on occasion, I had things wrong before. I read situations wrongly. It had gotten me into trouble before, a lot of trouble.

Still, I felt sure I was right this time. I decided to look for a sign the next day, a sign I was absolutely right. Just for my own peace of mind, if nothing else.

As it turned out, I didn't have to wait long.

"Miss. Cleve, if my wife calls… please tell her I'm busy," he said as soon as he came into work. He swung his case four times. A sure sign.

"Of course," I said. "Are you… Okay?"

He waved a hand at me and laughed. "Fine, married life, that's all."

His tie pin was crooked, and his shirt was creased. I left my desk and walked towards him. He flinched and stepped back as I tried to straighten both for him.

He doesn't want us to be seen, remember! No one can know! Especially now.

"Sorry," I mumbled.

"That's fine. I appreciate it. My wife's at home all day, but she doesn't know how to iron!" He attempted a laugh and failed while my mind raced.

Our code! He's telling me she's at home. I know it!

"Oh and, could you get me a coffee?"

"Sure," I winked.

He retreated into his office, looking a little dazed. I felt bad for him. He wanted his wife to be murdered. That had to be tough. But I understood him. On a deeper level, I wanted his pain to stop. Once we were together, I felt sure I could make him happier. I went to make him his coffee and thought hard.

So, I need to say I have an appointment. Or a meeting? No, an appointment. But where? Doctors? No, dentist.

"Would you mind if I pop out for an hour later? I have a dental appointment," I asked him.

"Of course you can. Take as much time as you need."

He's telling me not to rush things, to be careful.

"Thank you."

I left him bent over his paperwork. He clicked his pen three times. Excitement filled me. That was confirmation.

Once she's out of the way and he's officially grieved for a bit, we can be together. Just me and him. Finally, I'll be loved.

I felt overjoyed. I smiled all morning and counted down the seconds. By eleven, I couldn't wait any longer.

I wasn't thinking much about alibis or the fact my car might be picked up on security cameras or traffic cameras. The vision of me and him filled my mind and stayed wedged in place.

He'll cover for me. I just have to trust him. He loves me. He does. I need to do this because he can't.

I left and quickly called at one store. I paid cash for a set of large kitchen knives.

On my drive over to his home, I picked out wedding dresses and bridesmaid colors in my mind, styles of rings I liked, and where we might take our honeymoon.

I was so lost in my wonderful thoughts that I almost drove past his house. Quickly, I reversed and parked doors away.

The street was fairly empty, so I decided to go around the back way. I headed to a side gate, it was locked.

He should have found a way to keep it unlocked! Oh, maybe he did, and she checked and locked it. That must be it.

I climbed over a short gate and landed with a thud.

My heels! Take them off.

An amateur mistake. I found myself in a passage to the garden. I snuck around the side of the house until I was under the kitchen window. I could hear music and voices.

Shit! Now what? Does she have people over?

It was the phone, she was on the phone. I risked a peek and saw her. She stood with her back to me in a large modern kitchen, chopping exotic fruit as she spoke. All stainless steel and polished metal and her. Her vile voice and stupid hair.

That's the first thing I'll change when I move in. That kitchen, yuk. It's far too clinical.

"Yes, yes. Just give me an hour and I'll be there," she spoke into the phone. Then she laughed, a disgusting high-pitched laugh.

Carefully, I pulled the handle on the back door. It wouldn't move.

Just knock and kill her. Just knock.

I waited for her to finish her dull conversation. I stood and knocked twice. She jolted and spun towards me. Her eyes met mine and narrowed.

Bitch.

"Hi!" I grinned. "My child's pet rabbit escaped. I think it got into your garden," I shouted and pointed wildly behind me.

She made no move to come to the door.

"Rabbit?" she said. I could only just hear her through the glass. Her eyes were full of confusion and uncertainty.

"Yes! I'm sorry for trespassing, I'm very worried about the rabbit."

"My husband is upstairs," she said. Liar.

He'll be my husband soon, bitch.

"Oh yes. That's Micheal, isn't it? I'm new in the street, but he knows my husband. He's a lawyer too."

Her shoulders visibly relaxed. A smile began and lit up her face. She crossed her kitchen in a few steps and opened the door wide.

Do this, do it for him and for me. Free him.

"Sorry," she said. "I didn't mean to be rude, I just didn't know…"

The knife went in easier than I imagined it would.

I aimed for her heart but hit her upper stomach. Her white shirt quickly turned red. I stabbed her again as she crumpled, shock and pain all over her features. Down she went, easily. I plunged the knife into her back again and again. She lay gurgling, eyes wide open. She made a vague attempt to crawl across the patio and then she stopped entirely. I raced into the kitchen, washed the knife, and left it in the sink. I found my shoes, climbed the gate, and out. Back into the street as if nothing had happened.

The only detour I took was to call at my flat to get a clean blouse. I made it back to the office in no time. I'd been gone one hour and forty-two minutes. Not bad at all.

"How was the dentist?" Micheal asked me.

I knew what he really meant was to ask if everything went as planned.

"It went well, very well," I assured him.

It's our code, he'll understand. He knows.

He clicked his pen twice and nodded.

I sat down at my desk and got on with my work. At just after four in the afternoon, all hell broke loose.

I heard the ping of the elevator. I looked up to see three police officers heading straight for us. Two detectives walked behind them, a serious-looking man and a woman with steely, cold eyes. The kind of eyes that like to peer into people's business.

They're coming to tell him. He'll have to act surprised. He'll have to cry and scream.

I had faith in him, I had the confidence he could pull it off.

Come on Micheal, you can do this.

My heart soared, I felt proud of him. The office door opened, and they came straight for me.

They handcuffed me. Forced my face down onto the important paperwork scattered across my desk. There was confusion, shock, and awe. They called my name over and over. Someone screamed. Me, I think.

I couldn't straighten my thoughts. They led me away. I heard Micheal wail in horror.

He's upset they caught me. It'll be fine. Or he's acting, re-member.

In the backseat of the police car, I told myself Micheal would get me out of this, somehow. In my prison cell, I waited for him. I waited for him to tell them it was all a mistake. I waited for him to save me as I saved him. He didn't come. I wouldn't speak. I wouldn't betray him. My probation officer arrived.

Cornered, I told them everything. They all had plenty to say to me too.

They told me I am unhinged, they said that my mind is sick.

They said Micheal had no idea of our secret, our signs, or our code. He told them he hardly knew me and that he didn't love me, never encouraged me.

They said that I am delusional and dangerous. They said I was a stalker, and that I had done it before, been in trouble before. Only those parts were true. I read the signs wrong before.

They called me a murderer. A cold-blooded killer. That was wrong. I was an assassin. He was trapped, I freed him. He was supposed to be mine, and couldn't they see how my blood boiled red hot? Far from cold-blooded.

They said the signs and codes were in my head, only make-believe. Imaginary.

I have a cell, a room with four walls, and a bed. They make me swallow pills three times a day. They ask me how I feel, and they tell me that I am not allowed sharp things.

Sometimes, Micheal visits me in my dreams. He watches me as I watched him.

In court, he told the judge he loved his fallen wife. He acted as well as I knew he could. He cried real tears, sobbed until his body shook. I was proud of him. Truly, he deserved an Oscar.

His eyes met mine as I was led away. He gave me that *look.* That particular glint in his eye.

I knew then.

I knew it was a test, and that I had betrayed him by telling them about us.

It was a test, and I failed. Still, he loves me. He'll forgive me and he'll come for me. He'll get me out. Any day now.

I know it, I just know it.

A THOUSAND CUTS

I suppose you might wonder what it is I'm doing here, crouching in the bushes, alone. It's almost dark and I have nothing but a brick and a sharp knife for company.

I'm waiting for someone. A particular someone. That must be obvious.

Still, no one can see me hiding. I'm happy to wait. I have plenty of patience.

I have a secret, you see, a problem. A specific addiction that I can't seem to quit. It isn't drinking or drugs, it's not gambling or sex.

It's penises.

Or to be exact, severed by myself, penises. I know how that must sound coming from someone like me, a happily married suburban housewife with two teenage boys, a six-year-old daughter, a dog, a cat, and a guinea pig called Marvin.

You must have seen the headlines, the vulgar eye-catching titles. 'Penis stealer strikes again!' or 'Vigilante attacker praised by internet.'

And my personal favorite, 'Scent dog finds rogue testicle.'

My fault. I whipped a testicle off quite by accident on the night I used my garden shears instead of a knife. Damn thing flitted off into the bushes, lost until the dog found it.

You must already think I am utterly insane. We judge after all. It's what we do without even thinking about it.

At least let me explain. Let me start at the beginning. But I'll have to be quick, I'm cooking fajitas later and I have to pick the boys up from football practice.

I kind of witnessed a crime when I was seven years old.

Our next-door neighbors, the Williams, were good, nice people. Except, Mrs. Williams was prone to inviting the postman inside her home. Only when Mr. Williams was out, of course. One day, maybe he suspected, who knows? Well, one day, he drove away and then returned thirty minutes later.

The postman was in his home and likely in his wife too. He killed them both. I heard the screams as I sat lining up my dolls in the order I liked the best. Later, I heard the sirens and commotion. I asked my mother what had happened.

She told me that sometimes, life was like a thousand cuts and that having those cuts happen all at once was just too painful for some. She said it makes them snap.

After that occurred, life carried on steadily.

I grew up. I found a good job I half liked. I worked hard, I socialized.

I met a good, kind man, he became my husband. I gave birth to two healthy boys, then a girl. I became a housewife, a role I was content and happy with.

I cooked, I cleaned. I ironed, I washed. I ran the home. When the boys started school, I joined a yoga class with an onsite playgroup. I learned to grow vegetables in our garden. I planted pretty flowers and learned how to preserve food. I made friends. Good ones. I started a book club, an actual book club with five members.

I went through much of my adult life with blinkers on. Tunnel vision. Crime was something that happened on television shows. It didn't happen on my street, in my town. My friends and family were safe. Until the day they weren't.

I had a friend. I'll call her Leah.

She was a happy, bubbly kind of soul. She always had a kind word for someone, always doing other people favors. She was always smiling. Until she wasn't.

I hadn't seen her for two months by that point, although I'd called her and knocked on her door repeatedly. I finally caught sight of her coming out of our doctor's office.

"Where have you been?" I said. I took in her appearance. She looked exhausted, bone-thin, and sick. "Are you ill?" I added.

Oh my God, she's got cancer, I thought.

No, not ill, but suffering deeply all the same.

I expected her to tell me she was dying given the look of her. I suppose she was inside. Instead, she burst into tears.

We sat in my car while she explained.

There was a man. She went on a date with a man she met online. They'd been talking a lot, he was nice to her. They met in a public place, all very sensible and safe. Except, he drugged her drink in a busy bar, drove her to his home, and raped her.

She ran in the morning, fled in fact. It was seven days before she found the courage to contact the police. She blamed herself. She had no proof. The police, although they believed her, couldn't press charges.

She told me she was leaving our town. Said she couldn't face seeing the man walking around, happy and punishment-free.

She bumped into him in a supermarket. She froze while he laughed.

The sparkle she always had in her eye had been stolen. Her wonderful smile broken and vanished.

"It's not your fault," I told her. "Who is he? Other women should know to avoid him. We can do something about this. Please."

I wanted to take on her pain, or at least, try to ease it. I wanted to stop it from happening again, to another woman.

In my mind, I made a plan to contact my single friends and tell them to steer clear of his particular profile. I felt appalled, shocked, disgusted. I wanted to help her, support her. It seemed to me as if she'd had her thousand cuts in one go many times over.

She was intent on moving away. Pushed out of her own town, out of her own home, by him.

It wasn't until I got home that the feeling of anger and rage kicked in something fierce. The more my mind ticked over, the more fury I felt.

Who the hell does this guy think he is? Getting away with something so life-destroying? I have a daughter... how can I protect her from predators?

A terrible crime had landed too close to home. I went online, I looked at statistics, data, personal stories from all over the world.

I ran to the bathroom and vomited, disgusted with myself for being so ignorant.

It seemed I had been living with my head buried in the ground.

I channeled my fury into my ironing pile. Cleaning and housework always did soothe me. My rage only increased. Inside a whirlwind of hate grew.

My husband came home, and I told him all about the crime. I kept Leah's name out of it. I have always been skilled at keeping secrets.

"It's sad, but it happens, I guess. Women should be more careful," he said.

Women should be what!

"We're not the problem," I shouted. "Why do women always get the blame? It's the way we dress, it's the way we look, it's the way we act. It's never men, is it?! Because you lot can't control yourselves! Men need to be educated! We raise our boys to respect women at all times and they do!"

Feelings I never knew I had began to surface. My hands shook with rage. I wanted to run into the street and curse every man who ever existed.

"Calm down!" My husband said. "It's not all of us. Some men are bad, some women are too. It's wrong but… Society is a mess. You're no one, you can't change anything."

I knew he was right, in a way. The majority of men we both knew were decent, good men, as far as I knew.

Still, he was wrong about one thing. "I'm no one?" I asked.

"I meant… I mean, you're wonderful, but not in a position of power I meant."

"Doesn't it bother you?" I said. "That a few rotten men make all of you look bad?"

"Yes," he answered. "But what can I do?"

No, it's not what you can do, it's what I can do.

A fire was rising inside me. One even three glasses of wine couldn't extinguish. That night, I stared at the ceiling, wondering how I could get into that impossible, far-off position of power.

Just two weeks later, I was knee-deep in trying to start a campaign for local bars to have the means to test for date rape drugs, when I heard a woman had been attacked in the park. The local one that runs by the canal. The park we visit in summer to enjoy the sunshine. The one my children have always played in.

The need to act became urgent.

I spoke to a few female friends, single ones, married ones. I wanted to organize patrols, vigils. I wanted to set up neighborhood watch meetings. I wanted women to carry whistles, hell, even fog horns if necessary, considering our country wouldn't allow any of us to carry anything to defend ourselves.

"No one pays attention," a friend said. "If a house alarm goes off, or a car alarm. I don't even look out of the window. If I hear a scream, I just assume it's kids just messing around."

The others said virtually the same thing. No one cared unless something happened to themselves or their family and no one ever thinks it will.

"Leave it to the police," my husband said. "You're not Batman! You can't go dragging people on vigils looking for crime. Stick with your book club."

I ignored him.

I couldn't ease my fury. The injustices ate away at me. I couldn't sleep. I couldn't concentrate. I itched to do something. Anything.

What can I do to make an impact? What can I do, really?

It was only when I was out in the garden deadheading my roses that I hit upon an idea.

My husband had always been a heavy sleeper. A snorer too. It wasn't unusual for me to get up in the night and creep downstairs to sleep on the sofa. It was so common that I even kept a spare duvet downstairs.

On a quiet Wednesday night, sick of trying and failing to sleep, I crept down.

The sofa was not my aim. First, I dressed in dark clothing. I swiped my best carving knife from the kitchen and rummaged in my carefully organized drawers. I went out of the door and out into the night.

I knew where the man who hurt Leah lived. She told me his name; the rest was easy. It wasn't far. I'd driven past a few times already. I looked for security cameras, signs of him owning large dogs. He lived all alone. Lucky me.

I walked along the streets, my hoodie up like a regular criminal. I saw no police cars, although they had promised to patrol the area more.

I don't know what my intentions were. I think it was mostly to teach him a lesson. Give him a scare or make him think twice.

I let myself into his small gate and went around the back.

His house was quite smart-looking. A new build. Small too. He had a narrow back garden and overflowing rubbish bins. One dim light was on upstairs.

I tried the door handle. Locked. I tried the patio doors. Locked.

Ha! Ironic to be a rapist and yet worry about your own safety.
I was going to walk back home. I swear it. I was.
A rock caught my eye. An out-of-place rock.
That's the kind people put spare keys in! A fake rock or stone.
I picked it up. I was right, it was made of plastic. Inside was a key. It was fate. I let myself inside.
He caught me sneaking across his creaky landing.
"Who the fuck are…!" He yelled before I smashed him over the head with a heavy vase that had found its way into my hand.

Cable ties linked together worked perfectly on his ankles and wrists. He had a nasty head wound, enough of one to render him briefly unconscious, but not enough to kill him.
I waited patiently for him to wake.
"Did you rape her?" I asked.
"Who?"
Don't say her name! He's bound to know. Still, she's left, she'll have an alibi. No one will think to link or suspect me.
"You know who."
"No."
"Liar," I said and held up my knife. He tried to squirm across his carpet like a tiny caterpillar.
"Okay okay! I'm sorry," he cried.
"So, again. Did you drug her and rape her?"
"Which one?"
Acid rose in my throat and chest until it burned. A red mist settled in and wrapped its tendrils around my mind.
I thought of all those lives he'd ruined. All the misery and pain he caused.
I lashed out and kicked him in the face. I grabbed his greasy hair and slammed his head down until his eyes closed.
Something took hold of me. A need I couldn't fight. I was lost in an absolute frenzy. I pulled down his old sweatpants. A shriveled tiny penis sat curled up, withered away.
There's the culprit!
Although of course, it wasn't, not really. It was his sick mind that was to blame. Still, I decided to remove temptation.
Grateful for the gloves I'd chosen to wear, I began to cut. Six deep slices in total. Skin and gristle, blood and nerve. It was squishy under my grip and difficult to hold. It was a little like cutting our Sunday dinner joint, only tougher.

Still, off it came. I popped it into one of my freezer bags. I didn't want them stitching it back on.

I always told my children, if you can't behave with something, then you shouldn't have it in the first place.

I ran down his stairs and left him in a growing pool of blood.

He'll die. I'm not a murderer.

I picked up his landline and dialed nine-nine-nine.

"There's a man injured," I said and gave his address.

"Where is the injury? What happened?"

"He had his thousand cuts," I said. "All at once."

"Pardon?"

From upstairs came the most terrifying, brutal scream I had ever heard.

I put the phone down, wiped it, and off I fled into the night with my prize. My trophy.

I pickled it.

I had plenty of jars and supplies. I pickled it and placed it on the top shelf in our pantry. I always loved making jams and pickling gherkins. None of my family ate them. Mostly, I made them for summer fares at the park. I knew it would go unnoticed. I lined it up, just so, how I liked it, and I smiled.

I put my clothes in the washer and put my nightgown back on. I lay on my sofa, my precious family asleep upstairs.

I couldn't stop grinning. The sheer power I felt. I wasn't a criminal; I was a vigilante. I was getting justice when no one else could or would.

I felt alive. Blissfully, truly alive.

I wasn't worried about fingerprints. I wore gloves. I wasn't worried about being seen, I wore a hoodie and he never saw my face. My voice was recognizable, but they'd have to suspect me to connect me.

The only thing that really bothered me was the fact that I had enjoyed, no, loved the experience. I had never felt so beautifully primal. I had avenged my friend. A woman, me, a housewife with a book club, had gotten the better of a very bad man.

In the morning, I made breakfast with a smile on my face. I hustled my husband out of the door and my gorgeous children off to school. I cleaned and scrubbed, I sang and danced around. I felt deliriously happy. Powerful.

I waited.

News came at just after two on the local radio. A man had been attacked in his own home by an unknown person and the circumstances were highly unusual.

Okay, he's alive. He lived. Good.

Rumors soon spread. People soon heard the gruesome details. I listened to all the gossip with a delighted glee.

So, that was how it started. Just over two years ago.

Right now, as we speak, there are eight pickled penises on my very top shelf, lined up, just how I like. I need more. I want more.

I promise myself I will stop when I get to ten and then I will destroy the jars.

I am a liar. I can't stop. I won't destroy them. They are my collection.

I scour news articles looking for men that deserve a visit. The ones who deserve their thousand cuts all at once.

I prowl the dark web and lure newly released pedophiles. I drive to other cities. I am careful. I am quick. I am ruthless.

I never go after the accused. Ever. Only those proven absolutely guilty or awaiting charges. Some I want, I cannot get to. Maybe one day I can.

Once, last year, a man died. I should have mentioned that. But really, it wasn't my fault he bled to death before the ambulance arrived.

The police know the vigilante is a woman. In two years, that's as far as they have got in their investigations.

I have never been suspected. I have never been questioned. I am an ordinary housewife. I cook, I clean, I wash, I iron. I do yoga. I have a book club.

Tonight I am making fajitas and picking my boys up.

I do not think endlessly over why I do this. There are arguments for and against. Many will say I am as bad as the men I take from. Think about this, I wouldn't be cutting through the squishy tissue and nerve of their most cherished body part if they chose not to rape, chose not to attack the innocent.

Some men, a rare few, think they are above women. They think they can hurt us and get away with it.

Let me tell you they won't. They beg, they cry, they plead. Two even begged for their own mothers and most of them pissed themselves in fear.

I choose not to have sympathy. I slice, I cut, I chop. I take.

I am keeping women safer if only by a little. I am keeping my daughter safe.

I have no regrets, not one.

Hush, he's coming. I can see him jogging towards me, sweat pouring down his shirt. He jogs twice a week. This is the fourth time I've been here, waiting for privacy.

This guy, he's a convicted pedo, he's been in prison, twice. Recently, he's been in trouble again for flashing little children.

I stand, I'm ready. It's almost dark, it's winter. There's nobody around but me and him.

I'll make sure he never flashes anyone ever again…

HARVEST

Our village has secrets.

Twisted secrets that grow hateful in the whispers of darkness.

Our village has land.

Strange land, sometimes bountiful, sometimes barren.

It all depends on how well we've behaved. How much blood has been shed to nourish the dry soil, or soaked into the heavy weeds and spiteful thistles that grow in a mean tangle of knots.

Our village has order.

Rigid instructions and tight rules of operation.

The land is wrong. It is thirsty and cruel. A mistress of terror with an insatiable appetite.

Our village is overlooked.

In old times, before our kin settled, people were slaughtered here. The land watched our pitiful human war without mercy. It saw us behave without remorse and it learned from us.

Out of the remnants of much death, the land created a female form from a fallen woman, a slain woman. She was birthed, half conjured from the ground itself.

Something new was born, or made, created.

We call her Solulke. Our true mother. Our unmerciful queen.

Some say she is something old, rose anew, others say she is something ancient reawakened. Or the last member of a subterranean race long forgotten, only alive in myth and legend.

Her grip is tight, and her needs are relentless.

Her tithe must be paid. Her fierce hunger satiated.

It was my turn to place the posters along the main roads, my turn to hammer the sign with its sharp and pointed, wooden end into the ground.

'Free food and lodging. Good cash pay. Two weeks manual work guaranteed. Apply at Queens Orchard. No references required.'

Of course, no references were required. Hardly anyone in our village cared who came, only that enough arrived.

I cared. I cared a lot.

The sign and posters all carried the same advertisement. A waterproof promise handwritten on canvas and card. I understood that turning sixteen meant that I had more responsibility. It also made me more complicit. It felt like a step too far, and one in the wrong direction entirely.

Still, there was no choice. Not really, and if there was, I could never see it. I hardly dared to look.

I left in the truck I wasn't legally allowed to drive and headed down the complicated spiral of dirt tracks away from our village.

We were eight miles away from the nearest town, although it could have been a thousand miles.

My kin had lived on our land for hundreds of years or more. It was truly ours, in a way. Still, we were labeled as a cult by outsiders and largely avoided.

This suited us. In fact, we depended upon that rumor. We depended on being left alone.

We were all educated in the ways of the world. We knew all about religions, wars, pollution, and politics. We knew most people worshipped new gods.

Neon gods of billboards, technology, reality shows, social media, and themselves. We knew it was a strange yet extraordinary world run by outsiders. Our village members wanted to be separate, they were glad to keep the world at arm's length.

I, for one, wondered endlessly of the lives beyond my grasp.

I bumped along the track, thinking hard.

A large sign that had been standing since before I was born pointed the way back to our home, Queens Orchard. I drove past it, out and along onto the main roads. Occasionally I stopped and stapled posters to telegraph poles until my collection of twenty were used up and displayed. I hammered our sign into the ground as hard as I could.

People would come. They always did, although it was getting harder each year.

Reputations spread, after all. Words and suspicions had ways to travel faster and further in the age of technology.

Still, we genuinely needed people.

The fruit of our orchards had grown wonderfully. Ripe and beautiful. As soon as we had the help to pick them all, my pa would be making the long drive to the fruit buyer and seller. Our peaches alone were the stuff of legends. Both greatly sought after and admired. Our grapes made special wines. Expensive bottles designed to sit in the cellars of the wealthy, made only to collect dust and value.

Being away from our land started to hurt me.

A sensation pulled deep in the pit of my stomach. The land was my anchor to the world, and I was told it always had to be that way. The tie that bound me.

Over the years, I had grown to accept the need to be home on our land, until a small part of me rebelled. A glimmer of consciousness, a ripple inside myself, a spark of wonder.

I knew the further away I traveled, the colder I would feel. To venture even further would provoke agony. A wrenching white-hot pain in my mind and bones. A reminder from our true Mother to return, a sharp yank on the invisible chain I was born with.

But is it true? What if? What if I just keep driving and never come back?

I climbed back in the truck and drove straight home.

Two days later, a couple arrived. The woman wore a yellow sundress, one made of pretty loose fabric. I liked her smile. Her partner wore jeans and a smart shirt. He seemed quite at home in our rugged land.

They were greeted warmly and given bunk beds in one of our nicely converted barns.

They were traveling across our country and stopped to pick up work wherever they could. I liked them on sight, especially her, and that was a shame.

A day later, a whole group of seven arrived in a worn-out camper van. They were on their way to a place I had never heard of. They, too, were given beds, food, and smiles.

"Can't that be enough now, Mother?" I asked one night in our own little wooden cabin.

"No," she said. "And don't you dare say that again."

My stern mother was right, I suppose. I knew the number had to be eleven. The rules were set even before my own Great-Grandmother had been born. Deals made in bone and blood.

"And no talking to them," Mother reminded me.

I knew that. I knew I wasn't allowed.

Our village had thirty-two people in it, all made up of eight families. We could all trace our origin points back to the very first settlers on our land and the Celtic people before them. The first ones that made the pact, damning their following generations right along with them.

Our elderly women were the wisdom keepers, the holders of sacred knowledge. They were treated with great respect. Adoration, in fact.

We kept an acre for housing, consisting of small wooden cabins and clean barns. We had animals, cows for milk, and chickens for eggs. Our orchards spread as far as an eye could see. Then there were the woodlands. The tough terrain and isolated spots we were forbidden to wander.

We also had cave areas. Under the ground and on top, deep tunnels like honeycomb spread throughout the land and underneath our feet.

As soon as I turned sixteen, it was decided I would marry Six from the Wheat family that coming winter. It wasn't a bad match, we got along well enough.

I was working with Six, placing our freshly picked fruit carefully in special containers, when two more people arrived looking for work.

"That makes eleven," I whispered. Six nodded. He never spoke much, and that's what I liked about him the best.

I knew my mother would be pleased. She was the rule maker and village leader. Solulke's first in command.

A few moments later, my mother sought me out and ordered me to remove our signs. We needed no more workers to arrive.

I climbed back into the truck, drove, and removed every one of them. A small part of me longed to keep driving, just to see what might happen. The moment the thought crept into my head a strong pain hit that almost blinded me.

Solulke knew my idea in the same very seconds it had formed. Still, I placed my foot down hard. The crippling pain forced me to stop and pull dangerously over. I sat gasping for air, stunned.

She knows, my mind screamed. She knows!

I swung the truck around and headed home. The feeling of rage swarmed around me. I knew, sensed it wasn't my own, but hers instead. She was angry, furious with me.

At age twelve, I was taught our unique history. Our precious secret.

From that moment on, I knew what lived on our land. I knew what held us tightly in her grasp. I knew there was no way to escape her. She owned us.

A sacrifice had to be paid. One of flesh and blood.

Back at our village, all evidence of our signs removed, I parked up our truck and got back to work.

In the corner of my eye, I saw our new people laughing and chatting happily together. They would all be sleeping in the barn, in comfortable bunk beds, and they were bonding.

That worried me.

Part of me yearned to talk to them, to ask them about the world I never got to experience or see. The other part knew to stay away.

I watched the tall woman, one of the first to arrive. Her name was Lisa, I heard, and she worked hard. No complaining. I liked the way her hair swung and caught the sunlight. I liked her pretty blue eyes and her wide smile.

She caught me watching her and nodded. "Hi, what's your name?" She asked me. My mouth opened to reply. I managed half a syllable before my mother hauled me away.

"What do you think you're doing, Four?"

"Nothing," I mumbled. I kept my head down low to avoid her wrath. My mother could be cruel when she was angry, and she was almost always angry.

Four. My name was Four.

We were never given proper names until we were married. After that, we were allowed to choose our own. Until then, we were numbers. We were expected to be compliant, trouble-free, and meek.

I was dragged into our cabin by my hair. Mother stood glaring at me.

"I'm sorry, I was curious about them," I whined.

"You have aroused suspicions," she announced. "You foolish girl."

My eyes flew wide open and then I smiled. Suspicions? Why would the new people be suspicious of me?!

"Solulke demands to see you."

That wiped the smile off my face.

We were only one day away from the Solstice, our special day. The day of sacrifice and renewal. The day our true Mother is fed along with the land itself.

"But… I don't meet her until winter!"

Only women were chosen to meet Solulke, and only when they were married under the cold winter moon.

My stomach plummeted. I felt as if my intestines themselves had dropped to our wooden floor. Fear ripped through me. "I don't want to," I cried. "I'm not going."

"You must," my mother said. "She has called you."

This is because I tried to drive away. I tested her, and now she's testing me. This is my own fault.

I tried to act brave and fearless, like the women in our village were meant to be. The men were among us for breeding purposes and heavy chores only. Things were that way because our true Mother wanted them to be.

"Sunset. You must go to her," Mother said.

For a brief moment, I imagined my mother might feel sad for me, worried or concerned. In truth, I saw nothing in her eyes but spite. I had a feeling, deep inside, that she didn't expect me to return. I also felt that she wasn't the least bit upset about that.

I had to work for the rest of the day. I spoke to no one. I ignored one of the new people when he tried to smile at me and I ignored the girl, Lisa, when she brushed past me. Six ignored me too. He was solemn and quieter than usual. I expected word had already spread.

They all think I'll be killed for my mischief. For my tiny act of rebellion. Will I? Am I being sent to die?

Usually, I looked forward to nightfall. I liked to lie in my small bed and daydream about the world and all the possibilities it held. I had a magazine hidden under my mattress, one I'd found in the belongings of our previous year's workers. I'd stolen it before their possessions were burned. It had pictures of the world, images that stunned me. Beautiful women and gleaming massive houses. Cities and landscapes filled with people. I liked to stare and the photographs and imagine.

As our life-giving sun began to descend, a great feeling of nervous resignation filled me. As if I were off to the gallows to be hanged for my treason.

Mother came to pull me away from my work early and guided me close to the woodland.

"Find her, Four," she told me and gave me a hard shove.

I crossed the invisible barrier between our world and Solulke's. I entered a world that was entirely something of her own.

The chill of the woodland surprised me. The vast canopy of trees spread out over my head and filled me with cold. Her cathedral of forest, her secret church of nature.

I took small, measured steps. I wasn't sure how to find her, or where I was even meant to go. I stumbled and fell several times until my hands were grazed and sore. Each step forward caused more dread inside me, more terror.

What will she do? Will she kill me? I needed to know, I had to know the truth.

Before I was born, a woman from our village, one of her own, had displeased her. She was summoned and devoured, as the story went. Only scraps of her clothing and a pile of bones were ever seen of her again.

Will that happen to me? Shall I run?

I knew my idea was pointless. I wouldn't get far before I was doubled over in pain, crippled by hands unseen.

Outsiders can't help. They'd never understand or believe me.

I stopped and sat for a minute on a large flat moss-covered stone. I felt the velvet texture with my fingertips, pleased by the wet smoothness. My mind emptied of thoughts, and that's when I heard her.

Whispers. Her urgent whispers built up around me, luring. Half in a daze, mesmerized, I followed the sound.

My heartbeat raged a fury and my breath felt forced, harsh. I arrived at a jagged rock face with a half-hidden entrance underneath.

I could feel her. Calling me. Pulling me.

I squeezed myself through vines and bushes, fallen branches, and skillful camouflage. I scratched my skin and forgot to care. An urgency engulfed me, a need to find her, a brutal thirst written into the very code of my DNA.

"Solulke," I called. "I'm here." My voice shook with fear and betrayed me.

I blinked rapidly in the pitch darkness. I could sense her near me, assessing, waiting.

I heard a small scuffle and braced myself.

Soft yellow light filled the cave, lit from a source I couldn't find, and I saw her. For the first time in my short life, I saw her in all her twisted, wondrous beauty. I fell to my knees in awe.

How did I doubt? How did I ever doubt her?

At first, she looked like a large pile of rags moving all by itself. As my eyes adjusted, I made out features. Her form was human-shaped, but instead of legs, a thick mottled brown and green serpent tail whipped out behind her. One as wide as the tree trunks I'd passed by.

She had human hands and arms, slender ones just like my own. On the end of each finger sat a long vicious claw. She hissed and writhed, utterly powerful and superior.

Her eyes were two black slits, surrounded by a grass green color. Instead of a nose, she had two small openings. She used them to smell the air, to smell me.

Her hair was untamed, knotted, and wild. It spread out behind her like a rotten blanket. Small bones had been woven in that made her look even more terrifyingly beautiful.

Her mouth looked delicate. Until she opened it and roared. Row after row of brutally sharp teeth were revealed with two long lethal fangs.

Using her arms to propel her, she scuttled forward until her face was inches from my own.

I could smell rot and decay, but underneath sat the comfortable smell of lavender and the woods itself. Some of her skin was smooth and unblemished, the rest had scales like a fish has or a snake possesses. I couldn't take my eyes away from her.

"Solulke," I breathed.

"Four," she hissed.

For a few minutes, neither of us moved as we regarded one another. The fear inside me began to subside. A new feeling replaced it, one I couldn't fathom, one I couldn't quite understand the origin of.

Love.

I felt as if I were in the presence of something otherworldly and older than even time itself, in the presence of my true Mother, a divine being greater than anything I could have imagined. A living goddess.

"You wish to leave me?" Her mouth didn't move, but I heard the words all the same. Each one rattled around my head and echoed.

"No," I told her. "I don't want to leave."

It suddenly seemed absurd to me that I had tried to drive away, that I had tried to test her and leave her.

What was I thinking? What was I playing at? Why would it ever cross my mind to leave her? We need her, she needs us. We belong with her.

"I'm sorry. It won't happen again," I begged.

"Prove."

She reached up and stroked my face. I found myself longing for her touch, needing it. Tears fell from my eyes. With a quick movement, her forked tongue shot out and licked each one away. She took away my worry, my panic, and replaced it with clarity.

I felt overwhelmed with love for her, and it felt as natural to me as breathing. I wanted nothing more than to stay in that cave with her. By her side, no matter what the cost.

Can she sense how I feel?

I could sense her. She was giving me a chance at redemption, an opportunity to prove my devotion.

"Feelings are language," she whispered.

Gently, she leaned her forehead against my own.

I saw visions. Images and unknown scenes. I saw world after world, layered on top of each other, connected by cracks, leaking and seeping in. I saw a single lush tree bigger than the universe itself. I saw whole galaxies in her eyes. Canyons and odd planets, barren and rich. I felt her hunger, her desire to live. She dreamed a thousand dreams each night. She created and destroyed. She was both nothing and everything. Loving and indifferent, cold and passionate. A scene flashed, ancient humans, different to me, an origin point. A female battered, attacked. Her own child dead in her arms. Emotions of sorrow, fright, and grief. Despair. Blood on the ground. Muscle and sinew changing. Sleeping, waiting. More blood spilled. An endless amount. Twisted vines growing from the blood. Blackened and harsh. Then her. Her awakening as something different, something new. The fierce hunger. The yearning to thrive. The desire for chaos. She was the beginning. My beginning. My life. Not a chain around me, a connection. One that couldn't be severed.

I understood her. I understood her completely.

I woke from my daze, wrapped in her arms. As I moved, her clawed finger probed my mouth. One of her scales, from her body, was pushed inside. I jolted and coughed as the scale melted on my dry tongue. I swallowed greedily the taste of rich earth and soil.

She discarded me and scurried away, back into her darkness, her honeycomb cave.

I knew I had been dismissed. I stood and bowed, thankful. Grateful. Renewed in myself. New strength swirled inside me. New thoughts, a parasite of ideas latched on.

I left the cave a different person from the one I was when I first stepped in.

I also felt new knowledge in my mind. Something urgent. She needed thirteen, eleven would never suffice again.

As I left her world and rejoined my own, the village was quiet. Asleep. Time had no real meaning for any of us and I headed home expecting my mother to be sleeping. Instead, she sat in our small living room, staring at the empty wall, waiting.

"Well?" she asked.

"We need two more people," I told her. "We have to find two more."

"What!"

Our roles reversed and flipped. I enjoyed the feeling, I relished it.

"I said two more. Tomorrow, we find them, or two of the villages can have the honor."

"What happened?" She asked.

"I answer to her. Not to you."

"Four!"

"Two more. She needs them, Mother."

I walked across the room and into my small bedroom. I ripped up my illicit magazine. The world beyond held no interest for me anymore. I lay on my bed and dreamed of Solulke until morning came.

I was not allowed to be part of the precession the year before. Instead, I had watched hungrily from my window as our prettily dressed village elders led that year's workers into the woods. They had all been drugged. They each stumbled and clutched each other blindly. I'd felt a deep sadness for them all. Both pity and jealousy.

I pushed those thoughts aside and shook my head.

Everything is different now.

I gazed into the single mirror I had. My skin seemed brighter, my hair looked shinier, thicker. My eyes looked more clear, vibrant. I felt renewed, or brand new entirely.

She is mine and I am hers, my mind sang.

I knew within myself that my sudden change might seem abrupt, yet for me, it felt normal. Expected.

Fate or destiny, somehow. The love I had inside for my true Mother fuelled me until it burned.

With a passion none knew I possessed, I headed to the orchards and worked extra hard to please our Queen.

Six watched me with narrowed eyes and somehow, I found he had become irrelevant to me. They all had. A new power surged inside me, borrowed or found. I couldn't decide which.

An idea began to form in my mind, and I probed it, prodded, and explored. I tested my new connection to Solulke.

Shall I? Would it please you?

A resounding yes swept over me. Several other thoughts followed in a chain, and I held on tight. I decided things needed to change in our village. I felt certain our true Mother wasn't receiving the worship she truly deserved. I sensed her excitement.

I strolled through the last of the hanging fruits.

"Excuse me," the girl Lisa stopped me. "The fruit is almost gone, and we were promised two weeks of work. I'm just a little worried."

"Don't be," I grinned at her. "Tonight we have a party for the Solstice and then we need to plant and prune. There's plenty of work for weeks yet."

I didn't think twice about talking to her. They were my mother's rules, not mine.

Lisa was visibly relieved.

"I'll look forward to the party then!" She laughed. I laughed along with her, although my voice sounded empty and shallow.

I waltzed into my house intent on finding Mother. As expected, she was inside with two other elders, plotting and planning the evening's festivities, laying out her rules again.

"Get out, Four!" she shouted. "You're forbidden from this!"

'Take control,' a voice in my mind told me.

I stood up a little straighter.

"No. I speak on behalf of my Solulke. Tonight, you and Pa will join the others. She demands it," I said.

"How dare you!" Mother cried.

"She demands it," I repeated.

My Mother stood, already in one of her instant rages. She raised her hand and stepped toward me.

Our small cabin rattled. The ground vibrated and pulsed beneath us. My skin prickled with heat as I felt an unknown energy spark inside me. The feeling was glorious. For a brief moment I was Solulke, and she was me. We stood united in our joint demands.

My hair flew up around my head, full of static. My eyes burned like fire and took in every detail of the room, every expression of horror, every speck of dust on the surface and floor. I shuddered with power.

The two elders dropped to their knees, convinced. As did my pa. My mother, however, refused. Jealousy engulfed her expression.

"You've gone mad," she spat, eyes narrowed. "You speak for no one."

A voice that wasn't my own started up in my head.

'A small part of her never submitted to me. She desires more. She follows rules out of fear alone. She wants to control, dominate. She wants me to exist, not live.'

My right arm started to rise on its own. I watched it with a strange curiosity, as if my limb didn't belong to me any longer.

My hand struck and hit my mother hard. She fell, surprised, stunned, horrified.

"Bind her," I told the others. The words from my mouth were not my own. Solulke spoke through me. She used me as her voice, and I loved her even more than before.

I knew she wanted absolute devotion and, with me she knew she had it.

Who was I before her?

I found I had forgotten.

Hours later and I was dressed in a pure white gown of lace. It was supposed to be saved and worn only on my wedding day.

"There won't be a marriage now," I told two elders as I got dressed. They each nodded and accepted my instructions.

The punch had been prepared, one made with very special ingredients, just for our guests, and they were busy drinking their drugged, delicious treat. A bonfire was lit, others were getting ready for our special night.

I heard the gentle soft tones of a flute start outside. A flurry of excitement flared inside me.

Are those my feelings or hers? I searched myself for an answer and found that the emotion belonged to us both.

It begins. We will honor you as we should.

I opened the door and saw the faces of our villages. Some wore rapt expressions, some concern.

'Keep our secret,' Solulke told me. I counted heads. Twenty of us were under fifty years of age, the rest were over.

"Solstice! For our true Mother," I shouted. A chorus of clapping and whoops of joy greeted me as I beamed in pleasure.

If anyone despised my sudden takeover, none dared to say. Solulke would know which ones opposed in their mind. She knew everything.

Together, we joined in a line, held hands, and danced in a circle. Music played as we spun around the raging fire as one. Corn dolls were passed from hand to hand, the fruit was eaten and enjoyed. I laughed until my face hurt.

"Solulke, Solulke, Solulke," we chanted.

I felt dizzy with merriment, overcome with joy. A yank in my stomach pulled me back to reality.

'It is time.'

I addressed one of the elders, Mary. "Fetch them. Six, Matthew, Nine, Grace, Tom. Help her."

No one hesitated. I had expected resistance and received none.

For some minutes, we all stood still. The crackling of the fire and the muffled screams of our workers were the only sounds to be heard. They were led out of the barn roped together in a chain, stumbling and frightened, drugged and dazed. Condemned prisoners.

Mother and Pa were at the tail end of the human line, marked for sacrifice.

"This is an honor, an opportunity to belong to something greater than yourselves. Die with dignity, die with the knowledge that your death means something. You feed a mighty goddess, a living deity. Come!" I led the way with pride. I felt I was in a role I had been born to take.

Entering the woods reminded me of the night before. How I had crossed the realm a frightened girl and returned as something else. A true version of myself.

The path was treacherous. Our sacrifices fell, screamed, cried, and collapsed. Some had the strength to beg, to plead, or bargain. We ignored them. It happened every year, after all.

We sang old songs with pleasing melodies and drowned out their panicked cries.

At the cave, we stopped.

The chain of humans bound together fell to the floor in a tangle of limbs and tears. Lisa, the girl I had watched, fought hard. She kicked and lashed out and bit at her rope bindings. I felt nothing but anticipation.

I stopped forward and addressed them. My words ran smoothly, like velvet. Her words.

"For hundreds of years, Solulke has waited. Our true Mother waited for the right time to begin to rise. Every year eleven strangers have been placed before her. Now thirteen are brought. Solulke wishes to leave her cave, her underground. She wishes to walk under the sun, the stars, and the moon. She longs to be part of the world once more. She wants to live freely. Who here wants that for her?"

The crowd behind me muttered and jeered as I spoke.

"We have a great privilege. To stand by her side as she rises. She is unstoppable. She is our Queen."

I felt our true Mother writhe forward before I saw her. The branches outside her cave snapped and parted as if a doorway had opened. The bushes moved as if by their own accord. She was larger, more powerful, more otherworldly, and even more beautiful than before.

In all her glory and magnificence, Solulke roared. Her rags were gone. Her naked body moved as a serpent would. Her scales ended at her waist. Smooth skin followed, pert breast and gleaming skin. She hissed. The sound felt like music to my ears.

The sight of her made me breathless. Behind me, a few village members stepped back. Solulke snapped forward and fed.

The frantic screams of the sacrifices pierced my ears. Blood and bone flew as she devoured. Snarls and wet ripping sounds filled the woodland as she clawed and savaged, desperate for her human meat and souls.

One of our workers lay gurgling in fear. In a quick motion, she severed his head and swallowed whole. I saw it speed down her throat in a single gulp.

Intestines were strewn around. People behind me made retching noises and one even vomited.

She was glorious in her hunger. Magnificent in her power and strength. In her claw she held a liver. In one motion, she gulped it down with ease. Her body was saturated with blood. She shone with power. Thirteen dead.

She pointed at me, beckoned me forward.

With two hands, she held out a still quivering heart, riddled with nerves and thick chambers. Inside me, I knew it was the heart of my dead Mother.

'Bite,' she told me, and so I did. I bit, and I swallowed.

Our pact was made final in those few seconds.

The unbreakable contract between us. I was hers. My soul, my body, I belonged to her completely. She nodded, almost imperceptibly, and swept past me in a lethal movement. She struck the villagers, the ones who had opposed me, had opposed us in their minds and in their hearts. I knew to expect it, I kept our secret.

Seven of them lost their lives to her. Her serpent tail lashed out, spines broke, bodies shattered under her blows.

Three tried to run. She slithered through the forest after them, she enjoyed the easy chase and takedown. I watched through her eyes as she bit and tore. I tasted blood as she ate.

I was utterly in awe. I enjoyed their fear along with her. It fuelled her, powered her.

Solulke intended to rise someday soon. From those she devoured, her strength grew, her will increased, and I was fated to help her.

Forty-three of us walked into her woodland. Twenty-three returned.

In the days that followed, I laid out her new rules, her rules.

All of us twenty-three were her devoted, her congregation, her worshippers. I tasked each person with the job of bringing more people in, more sacrifices for our true Mother, our queen. I expected the police to arrive, and I knew exactly what we would do with them, where I would take them.

Once again, I climbed in our truck and stapled signs to poles. I knew more would come, and they did. They came eagerly and with broad smiles.

The chain on some of us loosened. A select few were given a wider berth to search for others. To snatch people for her. She hungers more in her need to flourish. We provide. She is inside me, all around me. I am her most devoted servant. I am hers.

Our village has secrets, and we hold them tightly. Beautiful secrets that grow in the darkness and in the light.

Our village has land.

Wonderful land, always bountiful. Never barren.

Our village has order. My order, her order.

Our village will never be overlooked again.
Her tithe will be paid in full.
She is risen.

GODS AND MONSTERS

Sixteen-year-old Ida Lambert pours hot coffee while she tries to fight her frantic heartbeat. A rush of flaming heat fills her cheeks. Her hands start to shake as soon as the diner doors open.

Keep calm, ignore them. She reminds herself.

She sees a group of students, the ones she tries so hard to avoid looking at her, whispering in hushed tones. The tallest girl giggles, a high-pitched fake shrill aimed her way.

Their gazes hurt her, mock her without words.

She knows they are laughing about her, talking about her. Making fun of her for working in the small student diner after classes.

They laugh at her clothes, her silent ways, her high grades, her hair, her lack of money, and lack of friends.

"You okay?" Her boss says from beside her.

Ida nods, not trusting herself to speak. A lump catches in her throat. It is not fear that causes her to behave this way, not shame, although her boss views her reaction as such.

It is rage. She hates them all, as much as they hate her or more.

Her boss, an older student, is astute. "I'll serve them," she decides.

She straightens her back and approaches the table, notebook, and pen in hand. Ida watches with narrow eyes, envious of her confidence.

She has a single class with the girls. One Maths class. She sits at the back and keeps quiet, pays attention while they laugh and joke together. There are four of them in total. Always glued together. A small coven of vileness.

On occasion, they throw things at her. Sharp paper airplanes or once thick chewing gum she couldn't remove from her hair.

The very moment Ida arrived at the school, they made her their target of hate.

Those girls think they rule the whole school. They think they rule over everyone.

One of the girls, Miranda, is the leader of the group, the instigator, the vilest one.

She has dyed her short red hair jet black. Dark kohl pencil lines her eyes. She is dressed in dark colors, with thick leather boots graced with huge buckles finishing the look.

She is trying to seem different, eye-catching, gothic, and mysterious. Instead, Ida thinks she looks desperate. She can almost taste her desire to be seen as unique.

Ida knows her change of appearance is to draw even more attention to herself. She knows she is a girl that craves to be admired, to be the center of worlds.

She's failed. Sent to boarding school instead of staying home. Another discarded student. She was sent out of the way like the rest of us.

Ida knows Miranda cries at night. She knows she sits on the edge of her bed and sobs, alone in her single dormitory room.

She knows Miranda often calls her mother and begs to let her leave the school.

Ida also knows the other three have secrets too. Twisted secrets kept from one another.

She keeps her head down while her boss takes their orders.

One more hour, she thinks. One more hour and then I can leave.

Ida does not have a wealthy family like the other students. Favors were called in to get her a last-minute place in the school. Her father views her as a disappointment and wanted her gone.

The only thing she enjoys about the experience is counting down on a paper calendar, marking off the days until she can go home, back to the rural building outsiders call a cult.

Deep down, she knows she is not welcome there either.

As soon as her shift is over, she heads across the campus. She walks with her head tucked down low against the steady rush of heavy rain.

Other students rush by her, she is ignored by all. Ida likes the anonymity in the crowd. She yearns for it.

She walks through the small quad with its wooden benches and moss-covered broken fountain. There are two separate dormitories, both attached to two separate schools. Sexes are segregated in lessons and rooming. For her building, an old sign announces *'Girls only.'*

She swings open the heavy wooden door and stamps her feet, careful to shake off all the rain onto the old mat. A few of her classmates are gathered in front of the old fireplace in the main lounge. A teacher, Miss. Alberts, tends to the flames. She also lives in the building. A constant presence, a spy, and breaker of illicit midnight feasts and meetings.

Ida ignores them all and heads up a twisting endless double set of stairs to her own tiny room at the end of the dark hallway. Ten doors line one side, eleven on the other, each one a single room.

A bathroom stands in the middle, a small room with three private showers. Each girl has a set time they can use the showers.

Ida's room contains a bed and a simple wardrobe. She thinks of the small space as her prison. In her three years at the school, she has not bothered to decorate it or put her own stamp on it as the other girls have done.

Ida visits their rooms every chance she gets. She likes to watch each girl as they sleep. She likes to wonder what they dream of, and think over who they are inside.

She knows the truth of a person is only ever revealed when they are alone.

She takes off her coat and hangs it on the back of her door. Without removing her damp clothes, she flops down onto her bed.

A whole weekend free. Where can I wander? Where shall I go?

Ida smiles. The whole campus is hers for the taking. She can do whatever she pleases, roam wherever she likes.

Ida closes her eyes firmly. She settles herself into a comfortable position and breathes slowly. She is a natural; she has the gift her father hoped she would have. Sometimes, she needs help to bring about what she feels is her special life talent. On those days, she cuts her skin deeply. She waits for the shock and pain to loosen some crucial part inside of her, the anchor that hangs in place and weighs each one of us down.

Deep breaths, in, out, in, out. She empties her busy mind.

Ida has trained almost her entire life. Her father and his group, the teachers. Rituals, Eastern philosophy, meditation, yoga, occult studies, even advanced physics. She grew up in an environment completely alien in nature to the western world she has been sent to live in. Her former life was with a group of fifteen carefully selected people, all intent on perfecting astral travel.

Not a cult, not to her. But a place for skilled people. People with a particular talent, a specific skill.

More breaths.

She feels the tension in her small body begin to ease, feels her mind empty itself. Feels a tingling sensation start at the top of her head, spreading slowly down to her toes. Heat bursts across her. Electricity and static. A jolt, a pull in her belly. She is lighter, she begins to rise. A disconnect, soul from body.

She rises higher, up from the bed. Away from her body. Out of her body.

She is free.

A silver cord connects her to her earthly self, thin and glittery like cotton caught in sunlight.

Ida does not have a heartbeat in her alternate form, yet she feels more alive. She does not have skin or texture, yet she feels touch more. She does not have physical eyes to see, yet her sight is perfect.

She is in the same world. A translucent form of herself. Her spirit, her soul, the energy that makes her *her*.

Unseen by human eyes, she leaves the room. Past a cluster of girls lingering in the hallway, girls who briefly feel the chill as she passes. Ida flows down the stairs and out. Walls and doors are no barrier.

For her, the world is gray now. Light is different too, it bleeds like watercolors in the rain. She walks on firm solid ground, a skill not many of the others possess. Most of her father's members can fly, float, or glide. Ida can too, faster than any of them, longer than anyone.

She can also interact with her environment. She can touch solid objects. A talent her father always claimed was impossible. Still, Ida can and does.

She crosses the quad with lazy steps. It's night, cold, but for her, it doesn't matter. A single girl walks past her, close by. She stops and shivers, wraps her coat more tightly around herself as she senses an otherworldly presence. Ida pushes on. Towards the block marked '*Teachers,*' in its old-fashioned calligraphy.

She drifts through the wall, solid is meaningless for her unless she chooses.

Her cord stretches behind her, follows her, coils in on itself like the tether of an astronaut.

She heads for one room. One old cold building where a single teacher sits marking papers.

The man does not look up. Too intent on his task, he focuses, head down, marking and commenting. Ida watches. Occasionally, the teacher grumbles and moans, whispers to himself. She waits.

She steps beside him to peek at the papers he discards. There, her name in block capitals. A second piece of paper covers her grade.

Slowly, she reaches. Pushes the paper slightly.

A! I have an A+!

There was no need for her to check. She already guessed her grade. Had already traveled in to memorize the exam questions before she took the test.

The teacher slaps his hand down on the table, he sees the moving paper. He stops, frowns at the closed window and tuts.

He scrapes his chair back and stands, crosses the room to search for drafts. Ida darts out of the way, stifling a giggle.

She leaves through the wall, the heavy stone wall, and back out. With a graceful push, she propels herself away from the ground and into the air.

Her tether follows.

She feels wild and free. She spins and dances, curls herself into a ball, and hovers. The night below her is full of tiny pinprick lights. A model village spread below her.

She pushes up towards the stars. Up, up, up.

A sharp yank stops her. She has reached her limit. The taut line of her cord offers no more resistance. She places her hands on the silvery thread and pulls herself back. Down, down, down until her feet land on the concrete of the quad.

One day I'll go further than ever.

Ida drifts in through the main door. She expects the student lounge to be empty. Expects that the teacher has hustled everyone to bed as usual. Instead, the four girls, the ones she hates, sit together around a small round table.

They are still. Not one of them moves. All eyes are closed. A single candle burns in the center of their circle. With a few more dotted around the room. Miranda, the alpha, Jane, the sweet shy type, Liz, Miranda's enforcer, and Grace, the smart one. A cliche group.

What are they doing?

She takes a few steps towards them and hears Miranda's hushed velvet voice.

"Is anyone there?"

Ida smiles. She knows exactly what they are doing, and she knows she can have fun.

She decides to act.

For a few minutes, she is simply content to watch the girls.

The Ouija board between them looks old and cracked. A thin line runs down the tarnished middle. The slender fingers of each girl are placed on top of the planchette.

"This is stupid," Liz says. She blows a strand of hair away from her forehead in frustration.

"Just wait," Miranda snaps back. "Be patient. This school is so old, it's bound to have ghosts."

Miranda clears her throat and tries again. "Is anyone there?"

Shall I?

Ida smiles as she steps closer. A candlewick flickers and registers her presence.

"Umm, guys. I feel like someone's here. Like, really."

Shy Jane has spoken. Her eyes widen as she stares around the empty room. She shivers deeply.

Concentrate now, feel the energy. Focus. They deserve a scare.

"Is someone here?" Miranda says. "Communicate with us."

Ida stands behind Liz. She cranes an arm between her and Grace and pushes the planchette slightly.

"Oohhh," Grace says and swipes her hands away.

"One of you idiots did it," Liz laughs. "I don't believe in ghosts."

"Keep trying," Miranda orders.

I'll move it again.

Ida pushed the planchette across the board and onto the floor. It falls with a clatter.

"Holy fuck!" Liz cries. She jerks rapidly, Ida catches her hair, and she screams. "Something touched me!" She wails.

Ida jumps back, clear.

The other girls are wide-eyed. Liz's hair stands on end as if lifted by static.

Ida concentrates hard. She extinguishes the candles one by one until the room falls into darkness.

She laughs as the girls knock chairs over in their stampede. All desperate to escape. She lashes out, her translucent arm pushes Liz.

Liz wails in terror. Bangs and cries cover Ida's laughter.

The main light fills the room and catches the four girls mid-flight.

"What are you all doing?!" The voice of Miss. Alberts. She stands at the foot of the staircase dressed in pajamas, her hair in a ponytail, anger across her face.

"Get to bed now!"

"But Miss!"

"NOW."

The four girls hold hands tightly. In a line, they follow their teacher like little ducklings. Ida sees that two of them are shaking. She likes it. Smiles contentedly.

Maybe this weekend won't be so bad after all. Lambs to the slaughter.

Once Ida's mind latches on to all the tricks she can play, she can't stop herself from dreaming up more.

Back in her body, back in her little room, she half dreams and thinks as she smiles.

Her father's lessons echo in her mind, he always had three rules to astral traveling.

Never stray too far. Never interfere with others. Never leave your body alone for longer than seven minutes.

Ida has broken all the rules repeatedly. She has never liked rules. Rebelled against them. It was one of the many reasons why she was sent to the boarding school in the first place, but not the main reason.

She checks the time on her small watch. Three in the morning.

I'm not even tired. Not one bit. I want to go again.

Ida knows she shouldn't. She knows, feels, that she can't bring the transition on naturally.

She switches on her lamp and rummages under her mattress for a knife. She pulls back the covers and examines the crisscross patterns of scars already present on her body. She seeks a tender spot on her thigh, one that might bring the most pain.

She slices deep and gasps, stifles a cry. Blood runs and pools onto her sheets. She arches her back and feels something loosen inside herself.

She breathes low and deep, forces herself. A jolt, a lift out, a push. She drifts up to the ceiling and through.

She stops, gets her bearings, and pushes out into the night.

She heads for Miranda's bedroom. Her light is on, the curtains wide open.

Ida hovers and peers in through her window.

They've all sneaked in! They're all scared! Ha! Good!

Grace lies on the single bed with Miranda. Liz and Jane are curled up on the small patch of free carpet, blankets covering them. They are all awake.

Ida drifts inside the room. The light flickers.

She listens and waits.

"I'll call her in the morning, I'm just going to say it," Liz speaks.

"Do you really think you'll be allowed to leave because this place is haunted?!" Laughs Miranda. "Maybe the ghost needs help. We should help."

"I'm not staying here! It pushed me!"

"Shhhh," hiss the others.

"I think we just need to calm down. It's not scary, okay. I mean, yes, I was scared, but it was just the shock. If we try again and…"

"Something's here," Jane whispers, almost to herself.

That's twice she's sensed me. How can she tell?

"What do you mean? Do you think you're psychic now?!" Miranda whispers.

"Something *is* here," Jane repeats.

The girls stare around the room. Grace buries her head under her blanket.

Ida begins to peel a poster from the wall. The sound fills the room and catches each girl's attention.

The poster falls halfway and hangs.

"Ignore it," Miranda whispers. "It's always falling down."

Lying bitch. Okay, explain this.

Ida flicks her wrist. The lightbulb above shatters. Glass falls down onto the bed. One girl screams, two start to cry. Miranda snaps her lamp on.

"Who's here?" She says, her voice shakes, and her eyes filled with tears.

Good, be frightened. See how you like it!

Ida drifts across the room and slams herself into the wardrobe. She hits it harder than she intended, powered by revenge. The bang is louder than she expected.

The sounds of screaming pierce her mind. She dives down and knocks pretty bottles from a dressing table onto the floor. She drifts through the window and spins, hovering.

The girls are running out of the door, screaming in terror. Lights are coming on all over the building. She follows her cord, races back to her own room and back into her body. She settles back in place with a heavy jerk, her thigh immediately hurting her. Her whole body feels slow and too heavy. She gasps with the sudden shock. A knock at her door jolts her.

"Who is it?" She cries, her voice breathless.

"It's me, I'm just checking everyone is where they should be."

The voice of her teacher, Miss. Alberts.

"Yes, I'm fine, I was sleeping," Ida shouts. "Is everything okay?"

"Go back to sleep," comes the gruff reply.

The next day, shaken students sit clustered around the breakfast table. Ida tries to wipe the smile from her face and struggles. She knows what she did was wrong, but not one part of her cares. She chews her toast to stop her mouth from grinning. Miss. Alberts appears and crosses her arms. She glares at each girl.

"I want no more repeats of last night! There are no such things as ghosts. Do you all hear me?"

"Yes, Miss. Alberts," all of the girls chorus together.

"And Ouija boards are forbidden. Whoever provided the last one should know that it's been destroyed."

"We found it Miss," Liz whines. "In with the board games."

A thick silence fills the air. No one speaks. An uncomfortable minute passes before the teacher leaves.

Ida peeks through her hair at Miranda and the others. They sit furiously whispering together.

They all look exhausted. Good. I should stop now. I've had my fun, my payback.

Miranda gets up and leaves the table. On the way past she elbows Ida hard.

"Sorry. Ugly bitch," she hisses.

Guess I won't be stopping after all. I'll stop when she does.

Saturdays are set aside for study. Each girl can choose to be in her own room or outside, on blankets in the crisp sunshine, or in the vast library.

Ida chooses to sit alone in her room. She doesn't need to study, she has access to all the answers she will ever need.

Instead, she lies on her bed and thinks.

What can I do? If I do enough, they might leave? Or at least, Miranda will. The bullying will stop. Especially if Liz leaves too.

Ida crosses the small room and glances out of the window. All the girls from her dorm are walking across the grass in clusters, little groups she will never be part of, all on the way to the library.

Do I have the energy to travel again? Yes, I'm a God, practically a God.

She feels untouchable. Feels as if everything she ever wanted is within her grasp. She lies on her bed as sunlight streams in through her too-thin curtains and breathes deeply.

It's against the rules to go so soon.

Ida pays no attention to rules. Within minutes, her body shudders as she leaves it behind. Out through the door, along the hallway with its multiple doors. She stops at Liz's room and drifts inside.

The room is neat, the bed made. Books are piled on a single shelf and the desk is organized, not a pencil sits out of place.

Ida reaches for a thick black marker pen. Her translucent hand slips through.

Come on, come on. I can do this.

She tries again. Her fingers tingle with effort. She has it. She grips the pen tightly and floats over to the wall.

She writes one word before the pen falls. She cannot pick it up, cannot find the energy inside herself to grip it once more. She wants to cause damage and realizes she can't.

Slowly, she drifts along the hallway and back into her body. She settles in, warm and comfortable. She sleeps.

Hours later, the sound of girls screaming wakes her. She jolts upright, for a moment, confused and disorientated.

"It was locked!" She hears Liz cry. "My door was locked!"

Ha! They found my message.

Sounds of activity outside her door, heavy footsteps, and more gasps of shock.

Ida waits and sniggers.

There is a knock at her door only minutes later. Miss. Alberts.

"Coming," Ida shouts.

Her limbs ache, her head pounds. She stands on weak legs, wobbles to the door, and opens it.

"Ida, did you leave your room today?"

Miss. Alberts face is pale, shaken. "No," Ida tells her. "I had a headache, I still do."

"Did you hear any noises at all?"

Behind the teacher stands the four girls, off to the side, peering and listening.

"Yes, actually, I heard some strange banging sounds. It woke me up, but I don't know what time that was," Ida lies.

The four girls gasp and mutter. Miss. Alberts watches Ida intently.

"There was an incident," she says.

"Where?"

"In one of the girl's bedrooms. Someone wrote on the wall."

"What was written?"

The teacher doesn't answer. She raises an eyebrow and assesses Ida.

She can't know I did it. That I wrote LEAVE. The door was locked. She can't suspect me, can she?

"It doesn't matter, Ida, I'll call the headmistress."

"Okay, bye."

Ida closes the door abruptly and thinks.

If they call my family, he'll know. Father will know straight away. Shit! Why didn't I think of this? Wait, why would they call him? I was in here, it's not a lie, not really. They can't do anything. As far as they know, I'm a good student. I work in the diner, and I've never been in trouble.

Ida shrugs, she lays back down on her bed and tries to sleep. She needs her energy for the night ahead.

As soon as night falls, she wakes. A bell, the sound of a bell has woken her.

Supper time.

Her stomach rumbles loudly, she decides to venture down. Saturday night is usually homemade pizza night, her favorite.

The hallway is empty when she leaves. Dark and sinister. *No wonder they all think this place is haunted.*

Ida is not afraid. She fears the living, not the dead.

Is everyone already eating?

She wanders down the stairs and into the dining room. The girls are all gathered into their usual groups. Cliques. Ida is not welcome to be part of any.

She takes a seat at the end of the table. Miss. Alberts crosses to her with a plate and pizza slices.

"I want you all to be aware," she announces to the room, although her eyes stray to Ida repeatedly. "There is to be no wandering tonight. No sneaking into rooms. I will be awake and in the hallway all night on the orders of our headmistress."

Ida isn't concerned. The other girls groan, whisper, and jostle each other.

This is good. I can scare them more if they're alone.

Ida covers her smile by taking a bite of food. She looks up. Miranda and the others are staring at her with narrow, vile eyes.

If looks could kill.

For once, Ida dares to stare back. The gaze becomes a contest between her and Miranda.

Don't look away. Don't look away. Vicious nasty cow, let her have a taste of her own medicine. Don't back down.

Miranda looks away. Ida eats more pizza with triumph.

Tonight is going to be epic!

Most of the girls choose to stay curled up together on sofas in the lounge before they get sent to bed. Miss. Alberts patrols, as if she is expecting intruders.

Miranda, Jane, Liz, and Grace sit in a tight circle around the table. Ida chooses to leave and heads to her room. She grabs her things and walks to the bathroom. She takes a shower, a long hot shower, enjoying the wonderful heat. The water drains her of tension. Usually, she feels unsafe in the shared bathroom, afraid others might see her scarred skin. She stands to luxuriate in being alone.

She doesn't hear anyone come in, doesn't hear the bathroom door open over the rush of the water.

When she steps out, towel wrapped around her, her gown has gone.

Written on the steamy mirror are the words, 'You leave, bitch.'

Very funny. Where are my things? Where's my gown? Those nasty girls. I know it's them. They probably think I picked Liz's lock to get in her room. Idiots. They have no idea.

Ida's towel only partially covers her scars. She realizes and, for a moment, panics.

Everyone will be downstairs. I'm only two doors away. Shit! I left my room unlocked.

Ida runs to the door and peers out. No one. She dashes to her room and flings the door open. Her room is in utter disarray. Clothes have been pulled out of her wardrobe; drawers have been yanked open. Her belongings lay scattered across her floor.

"Wait," she whispers to herself. "You just wait."

Ida can smell Miranda's perfume. She knows the damage has been done by her.

She knows she will not let her win.

I should have fought back a long time ago.

Quickly, she dresses in her pajamas and picks up her things. She wants to get in bed as fast as possible. She wants to terrify the girls, she wants Miranda gone by morning and Liz too.

She waits twenty minutes before the sounds in the hallway end. She wraps a cardigan around herself and leaves her room for the bathroom. As promised, Miss. Alberts is on guard duty. She has positioned a chair at the very end of the lines of bedrooms, at the beginning of the staircase. She sees Ida and raises a hand.

"Bathroom," Ida mouths and points. Miss. Alberts nods and goes back to her book.

I wonder if she'll fall asleep? All those hours ahead of her, watching doors. Shall I mess with her? No, I won't. She's never done anything wrong to me.

Ida uses the bathroom and walks back to her room. She locks her door from the inside and settles down on her bed, under the covers.

Her mind itches with the need to leave her body. Being out of body feels more real to her, more natural than life.

She feels for her knife, wedged under the mattress. She is pleased to find the cool metal still there and wasn't discovered by Miranda's rampage.

I won't need it tonight, just breathe. Breathe. Let go. Lighter and lighter. Free. No constraints. No weight, no burden. Only freedom.

The first time Ida left her body she was eleven years old. Her father had a lamp in his private study, the room no one was ever allowed to go into. On the lamp were symbols. Anyone in the vast house who achieved out-of-body-travel had to prove it. They had to know which symbols were written on the lamp. Her father was crafty. If one person reported back correctly, the symbols would be changed.

Ida's only aim in her short life was to find the symbols and tell him, impress him, for once, make him proud that she had achieved astral travel.

One night, after years of lessons and failing, she lifted up out of herself and out. She saw her body lying in her bed, she drifted through walls and saw the other house members sleeping. Ida discovered she liked to watch people in those moments. She made her way to her father's study and memorized the written symbols.

Inexperienced, she was yanked back to her body after minutes. In the morning, Ida did not tell her father.

She always intended to, but failed to say the words. She kept her secret.

Every night after, she would leave her body and take off by herself. She would roam the garden or stand quietly and watch the others.

She learned many things. Who was sleeping with who, which person loved another. She learned secrets and whispered promises.

Her father was disappointed in her claims that she just couldn't manage to leave her body. She had to study harder, meditate more, concentrate harder.

At thirteen, she left her body behind and visited her father's study once more. He was awake, and busy in a conversation with another house member, talking about her. Ida stayed to watch, to listen.

As he calmly smoked a cigar, he revealed he had decided to send her to boarding school. He was more than disappointed with her; he called her his biggest failure.

Anger rose inside Ida. Bitter sparks of fury erupted. Her father's cigar burst into flames. The leg of the chair he sat on collapsed.

Ida fled through the wall as shouts of surprise and pain rang out. She settled back into her body. Minutes later, her father peered in.

"Ida," he said in his gruff, deep voice.

"Yes," she answered, pretending to wake.

He closed the door quietly. He did not suspect her.

Two weeks later, Ida was sent to boarding school. On the rare occasions she was allowed home she was considered an outsider, not one of them.

She decided she liked things that way.

As she lies in her bed, her body begins to sweat with sheer force. She cannot induce a way to travel naturally. Ida reaches for her knife and seeks the supple flesh of her arm.

She slices, almost desperate. A vicious movement. Immediately, agony occurs. Ida gasps and feels a jolt inside herself, her anchor moving, her chain extending.

Come on, come on! She tries to breathe steadily and concentrate on the pain.

A heavy pressure fills her, the familiar lightness follows.

Yes! Yes, Yes!

She leaves her body, her earthy home. Rises up to her ceiling and laughs. She spins, as graceful as ever, and pushes out of the window and into the night.

For a moment, she hovers and gazes around her. No one is around. Just how she likes it. She flips in the air, swims as if she is underwater until her face is level with Grace's bedroom. She is asleep. Twitching and dreaming, a bright lamp kept on. She moves across Liz's room. A slight gap in the curtains, Liz is awake and reading a book. Ida concentrates and taps on the window. Liz jumps and screams, runs to her door. Ida giggles with delight and presses on.

Jane is standing at her window, staring out and frowning. As soon as Ida gets level with her face, Jane takes two steps back, her frown turns to fear.

She can sense me, I'm sure. She's different from most.

Ida speeds on. Her heart set on one destination. Miranda's curtains are drawn tightly.

Ida drifts through the wall, her tether trails behind her.

Miranda is sitting on her bed, awake and alerted by Liz's screams. No lamp, but candles. Seven candles, all white, surround the room. Miranda has a rosary in her hands, counting off beads and mumbling.

Ida floats close, she wants her to feel the chill her presence causes. Miranda stops her mumbling and freezes.

"Whatever you are, go away," she whispers. Her voice shakes with adrenaline and fear.

Ida focuses and causes one candle to extinguish. Miranda jumps as the wick hisses. A tear works its way down her face.

Don't feel sympathy. Remember everything she's done. I'll be happy when she leaves, so very happy.

Miranda's eyes dart to her door. Ida reaches out and pushes her.

She intended her focus to be a gentle shove. Instead, Miranda falls back onto her bed and bounces.

She screams wildly and throws up her arms, kicks, and lashes out. She scrambles up and falls onto the floor, caught and tangled in blankets. She throws them off in a frantic rush and races for the door. Ida follows.

Miss. Alberts is in the hallway, trying to calm Liz down.

"GHOST," Miranda shrieks and runs.

Ida laughs with glee.

"Stop! STOP!" Miss. Alberts wails. Liz grabs her teacher's arm and starts to cry. "Don't leave me," she pleads.

Doors begin to open. Sleepy, frightened girls poke their heads out.

Ida chases Miranda. At the top of the stairs, she grabs her tightly and spins her. Miranda lurches and falls over the teacher's chair. Ida lets her go.

Miranda is crazed, frantic with fear and desperation. Miss. Alberts comes running.

Miranda wails and pulls at her own hair. She scrambles up. For a moment, she balances, eyes wide with horror.

Ida watches in slow motion as she topples back and falls down the stairs. Down, down, down. Two flights of wooden stairs. She rolls at twists and screams until she hits the bottom. Her head lays at an odd angle, her eyes are open and wide. Blood drips softly from her open mouth.

OH SHIT!

For seconds, no one moves. Then comes the pounding of footsteps, the rush of activity, more yells and screams, quick orders are shouted. Ida leaves, out the front door and out.

Shit, I'm in so much trouble now! She's dead. I killed her! No, she fell.

Two sides of Ida argue while she fills with panic. She wants to get as far away from the building as fast as she can. So she can think straight, so she can settle and find a way to not blame herself.

She pushes off and over the quad. Over to the main school and onto the roof. It's a place she has found solace many times. City lights can be seen in the distance, the sight always makes her feel hopeful and excited.

Someday, she wants to live in a busy city, leave her body and wander every night. A million worlds and homes to see, a million people to watch. All those secrets waiting to be discovered.

Maybe Miranda isn't dead. Maybe she just, I don't know, has a few broken bones.

Ida knows her lie isn't true, she knows she's dead.

It bothers her that she doesn't feel troubled about the loss of life, she only fears being blamed or caught.

How could school find out? Only Father would suspect or know.

Ida fears the wrath of her father, she feels the wrath of the entire family. Sometimes she wonders if their strange ways and odd rituals make them a cult after all.

The sharp sound of sirens alerts her. Her silver cord, her precious tether yanks her hard.

Ambulances? Or police. I need to go.

Ida races back, a curious feeling begins to overwhelm her. She starts to feel cold. Brutally so. Her flight back to her body becomes a fight. Her translucent form begins to feel heavy. She watches, horrified as her tether judders, shatters like glass, and falls to the floor.

NO! No, no no!

Now it is Ida who is full of frantic panic. She hits the floor slowly and feels the shock, the pain of impact.

Is it my cut? Am I bleeding to death? RUN!

The closer Ida gets, the more she understands. The sirens belong to fire engines. The dorm rooms are on fire. Thick smoke billows out of smashed windows, blown apart by the heat.

No tether, am I already dead? Has my body died? Am I too late?

Clusters of students stand as a single hive mind, gazing at the flames licking the building away.

The candles, Miranda's candles. The realization hits her.

I'm dead.

Lights come on in every building surrounding them. People rush to help.

Ida sinks to the ground and cries.

Ida watches as her body is removed from the building, covered discreetly. Only two deaths, her and Miranda. No one could get to Ida, her door was locked from the inside, she wouldn't answer to the repeated pounding and screams of Miss. Alberts before the fire fully took hold and engulfed the rooms.

A student comes close, one Ida doesn't recognize. She lays a bouquet down as close as she is allowed.

On a bench nearby, silently watching, sit Liz, Grace, and Jane. They hold hands, joined in a chain, linked together, their leader, lost and fallen.

Ida does not know how long she has wandered, or how long it has been since the fire started.

Time feels different for her now. Still, no one can see her. But she can watch people to her heart's content.

For Ida, no white light opened up. No tunnel leading to Heaven or Hell. She wonders if she can walk to her home, and try to get her father's help, or if she has boundaries, limits.

She cannot decide what she wants to do or why.

Her feelings are dying. Her emotions are fading. Sometimes she feels the most vicious rage, sometimes she feels simply morose.

On occasion, she catches sight of others. Flickers of people, just like her, wandering. They pay her no attention. She wonders if they know they are dead.

Ida can still reach her private place on the roof. She can still drift through walls, but she must walk. She cannot glide or fly or float.

She likes to watch the city lights at night. She wonders what could have been. Sometimes she forgets where she is.

She finds herself wandering hallways and corridors. Sometimes she wails in pain.

She watches a new building rise from the ashes of the old. A phoenix building. One day nothing is there, the next, it is almost finished. Students come, some familiar, most not.

Ida feels a spark of memory as she watches a young dark-haired girl being teased by the others. She sits alone and friendless, sad and abandoned while the others laugh at her.

Ida decides she will not allow it. She decides she will act. In defense of the bullied girl, she will have fun.

Ida smiles.

JUDGMENT

They tell me I will go to Hell. Some even tell me I deserve a place in the fiery pits of eternal damnation. They say I should burn for my crime. That I should suffer even more.

They tell me death is my most just and worthy punishment. Some say my sin is beyond evil itself.

If I could have explained. If they had only let me talk, instead of confusing me with long complicated words and rules set in stone by them. Trial by fire. Guilty before my judgment even began. Seen and found lacking. Branded a vile woman.

My crime wasn't a sin. It was justice. It was pure survival. And now I face the ultimate punishment, a fate chosen by men.

A guard comes, he asks me which foods I would like to eat. As if a meal might fill the emptiness crawling around inside my stomach. I ignore him. Words feel too painful to form, too numb.

Another comes, he asks if I want to see a priest. As if a man of God might absolve me of my fear, of my terror. The kind of brutal horror I lived with for years.

I don't deserve to die, I know that. I deserve to live and thrive. Don't I?

My husband. The one who promised to love me always. Him. He wore a mask during our short courtship, played his illusions and clever trickster ways. I didn't see through his act. Couldn't. Love blinded me and, truly, I adored him. People called him a good man. They said I was lucky.

Our wedding in '52 was perfect. Joy filled me so much it hurt to breathe. My face hurt from my permanent smile. I was happy; we were happy.

Until it changed, he changed. His carefully constructed mask of deceit cracked apart like an old porcelain doll.

At first, small things. Angry words directed at me, followed by an apology and sometimes flowers too. Pretty scented roses, blood-red.

No marriage is perfect, I told myself. Persuaded myself.

He worked hard; I was forbidden from taking a job. I was meant to be a housewife. A rule laid down by him.

Every day, I would prowl our house, clean and cook, wash and fold. Nothing I did was ever right. The folds were wrong, the creases unacceptable. Food was overcooked, undercooked, tasteless, or sour.

"You're a bad wife,", he shouted. "Useless."

In my sadness, I vowed to try harder. I smiled more. I entertained friends of his by pouring drinks and serving food. A perfect hostess. I was dutiful, faithful, devoted. I wore the dresses he chose. Painted on the make-up he liked. Wore my hair just the way he wanted it. My wedding ring became a shackle.

Still, he was never pleased.

One sudden slap became two. A vile punch became a weekly event. Threats, manipulation, abuse. I couldn't see, I blamed myself. After all, I was useless, like he said.

I became pregnant. A child was born, a girl.

He wasn't pleased. Females had no value to him, only good for one thing.

Our daughter cried, teething. I couldn't silence her, she refused to be calmed.

A single blow, powered by frustration from his vicious fist, knocked me off my feet. I fell down onto the perfect tiles I scrubbed every day for hours. I knew then that one day he would kill me. I knew.

"I'm sorry," he said. "I'll change."

No emergency room visit. It was forbidden. Isolated inside our dollhouse of a home, I paced. I wanted to leave, to take my daughter and run. But to where? I had nowhere to go. No family, no friends, no job, no money, no hope.

Outside the front door, only shame and poverty waited to greet me. No life for my golden girl, my daughter, my reason.

No change in him occurred.

He stayed angry, primal with rage over my careless mistakes. One wrong word, a spill, a failure to do as he asked, provoked him.

He yanked my hair, threw me to the ground. Kicked, a brutal kick. Ribs snapped under his polished shoe.

"I'm sorry," he said. "This time, I will change."

No change.

Wounds took longer to heal. No rest. Hidden inside and imprisoned.

Pregnant again, forced every night. Another daughter arrived. Fury sparked inside him.

"It's your fault," he raged. "I wanted a son. I wish I'd never married you."

His wish was also mine.

Scarred, bruised, and ashamed. Time passed. Life drained out of me; the fight was already lost. Nowhere to go, no one to help. An empty shell acting as a mother, as a useless wife.

I paced again, a prisoner. Time ticked away slowly. I dreaded his arrival home from work. Still, I smiled, I acted. My turn to wear a mask. Anything to avoid his wrath.

On a hot summer evening, on our eldest daughter's third birthday, she spilled her milk as I cut her pretty cake. A simple accident. No harm done. None at all.

Enraged by the mess, he struck her. Hard.

A fire ignited, one inside me. My hands shook. My mind shattered, static filled my thoughts. A primal spark exploded. Rage of the kind I never felt before engulfed me. I snapped.

Knife in my hand, I stabbed. Again and again, one blow for each of mine. So many.

Warm blood and gore, the color of roses. Still, I stabbed, lost in a fury.

Then came screams, my own loud howls of horror. A sharp knock at the door from a worried neighbor. Then sirens sounded, gruff voices, the splintering of wood. Rough hands grabbed me. Pulled me away, away from my beautiful girls, away from the lifeless body of my husband. They put me in chains. A different kind to the ones that bound my marriage.

They called me a monster. They said my sin was beyond evil. They told me I will go to Hell.

It's almost time, and the fear inside me ripples. What will become of me? Where will I go? Those men that decided my fate, are they not murderers too? I don't understand. I don't.

I killed my enemy, like soldiers in a war. I was in a war too, a relentless battle. No bullets, no explosions, but a war all the same. I did not plot or plan. I did not poison or scheme.

Tears fall from my eyes. I am afraid of dying. Of what comes after. Will it hurt?

I have endured so much. I sought freedom. Freedom for myself and my girls. Instead, they served me death.

Victim or villain, they asked, while they had already decided I was the villain.

No justice. No compassion.

I killed a man before he killed me. I snapped first. A mother's primal instinct.

If I could only see my daughters one last time. If I could only tell them I did it for them. I wasn't brave enough to do it just for me.

What choice did I have?

I hear footsteps, keys jangling.

"Please God, no," I say. My voice wobbles and shakes with fear. My heart is racing.

Two guards, solemn faces. They have come for me.

I fall, scamper into a corner. I am so frightened. I know fear, I know pain. This, this is something entirely different.

"It's time," one tells me. An act of mercy, his eyes shine with tears.

"Please," I beg. "Please don't."

They glance at each other and step forward. I am cornered and I know it.

Trapped by men whose job it is to preach justice. A system in place, one designed back to front and upside down. Made by men as guilty as my own dead husband.

Keys click. My cell doors open. A resounding metal scrape pierces my brain. They grab my arms; my legs won't work. They pull me roughly as if I am a rag doll.

"Forgive me," I whisper. "Please, just forgive me."

I only sought life. I wanted to live without fear, without pain. I wanted to protect.

I only wanted to be free and now I die.

Down the bleak corridor, dragged to my damnation, forced into my ending.

Into the cold, ruthless chair of wood and steel. Strapped down by pitiless hands.

"Please," I beg. "No. Stop."

The same words I said to my husband, over and over. My fragile mind quakes. I feel the bindings in my brain fly apart. My mouth, rough fingers probe, and press.

I can't focus. Voices speak and I can't hear. My hair is pulled, a cap wedged on.

I need to tell them I am sorry. Sorry for saving myself and my girls. Faces watch, doll faces with cold glass eyes, no emotion. No regret. No mercy.

A countdown, a switch, a jolt of brutal terror with full power to kill.

And to think, I wanted to escape being murdered, only to be murdered by colder hands and hearts instead.

GLASS EYES

Ten-year-old Sally long ago decided she hates eyes.

Everything about them unsettles her. Her Grandmother once told her, 'Eyes are the windows to the soul.'

Sally doesn't understand what this means, but she thinks all windows should have curtains, for privacy, or at least, net ones.

Every night, her lavender-scented Mother settles her in bed and kisses her forehead tenderly.

"Night, night, little love," she likes to say.

"Night Mother," Sally always answers. It's a game.

Sally is clever. She knows her mother's words are forced, acted out each night. She sees the truth in her cold, cornflower blue eyes.

Sally frightens her. She blames Sally for what happened in the garden.

Once the main light goes out. The room falls into a strange kind of twilight state. A single lamp stands in the corner and casts bizarre shadows across the ceiling and plain walls.

She doesn't like the shadows. She wonders if they might thicken, come alive and gobble her up in one swallow.

Then there are all the dolls, well, the doll's eyes. She has more dolls than she can count. Her mother lines them all up so they face forward, always watching, never blinking. They sit on shelves aligned around the room, legs draped over, peering.

"They can keep an eye on you," her mother says. "And look after you."

Sally doesn't think the dolls have her best interests at heart at all and she doesn't want to see their souls behind their eyes, doesn't want them to see hers.

She glances at each doll in turn, as they each glare at her. Her grandmother gives her a new doll to add to her collection at least four times a year. A collection her father started off before he keeled over and died.

Sally pretends to be pleased and excited with every new doll, when in fact, she feels sick. The same kind of feeling she has when her mother drives over a small bridge quickly.

Some of the dolls are dressed in old-fashioned clothing, some wear pretty dresses. One is dressed as a harlequin clown and one wears the outfit of a chimney sweep, that one even has a tiny broom.

"They watch me," Sally once said. "I hate them."

"Nonsense," her mother answered. "They can't see, they have glass eyes."

For Sally, that made the dolls all the more frightening. She wants to poke the eyes out until nothing but gaping holes remain.

She squeezes her own eyes shut tightly and pulls her sheet over her head.

She hears movement.

Quickly, she pops her head back out.

She feels certain one of the dolls has moved. Feels sure they are conspiring against her, whispering evil plots.

Sally, terrified by the idea, lets off an almighty scream.

Her mother races up the stairs and into the room, frantic.

"What's wrong?" She yells.

"The eyes!" Sally sobs. "All those eyes!"

Sally notices her mother's skin is flushed. She has make-up painted on her face like a clown, with smeared lipstick around her mouth.

From downstairs, she hears the sound of a man's voice. Her stomach plummets.

"Sweetheart, John is here. We're having grown-up time, no more screaming, okay? The dolls are your friends."

Sally turns her back. She hates John. Creepy John, with his smells of oil and black-stained hands. Mother says it was because he is a mechanic, he fixes cars, the marks just won't scrub off. She doesn't like his eyes either.

He has the kind of eyes you shouldn't look at a little girl with.

Her mother closes her bedroom door softly and leaves her alone with multiple pairs of glass eyes staring at her. No, not alone, she has Bessie.

Of all her dolls, she only likes one. She's a special doll with secrets. She is the one her father brought home for her, when she was eight, a week before he died.

The black-haired doll is called Bessie and Sally takes her everywhere. She likes her eyes, brown ones just like her own, and just like her father's. The deep brown color of chocolate.

Bessie is carried to school, even though the other kids laugh. She sits at the table at teatime and sits by the tub when she has her bath.

Bessie hates John too. Bessie tells her this.

Sally lies awake and listens to the sounds coming from downstairs. Her mother's high-pitched giggles, the sound of deep booming laughter, the clink of glasses with grown-up drinks inside.

Her mother says John wants to move in. He gave her a cheap ring that turned her finger green.

Sally hates that idea of John spoiling her life more than she hates his eyes. When she said as much to her mother, her mother's own eyes narrowed. She got that *look*. That particular stare that meant she was unhappy. The look that meant she was going to cry until Sally had to say she was sorry, even when she wasn't.

Sally wonders if her own eyes are made of glass. She pokes at one, but it hurts and tears fall down her face.

She thinks about asking her teacher at school if she has glass eyes too, the kind one with the long brown hair. She knows that wouldn't be a good idea, she is already in trouble for asking weird questions and doing odd things.

It was only Sally and Bessie the doll that wanted to see what was inside the school hamster, only Sally that tried to look, tried to peer inside.

They all said it was because she lost her father so young, and that Sally saw it happen with her very own set of eyes.

They were playing catch in the small garden, her, her father, and Bessie. Father clutched his heart and staggered forward, down onto the grass. Sally copied him and fell. She lay as still as him, even Bessie joined in with the new game.

After a few minutes, Sally got bored.

When she shook her father, he was asleep. She wandered off to look for ladybirds. An hour later, she shook her father again. Still asleep.

Even her mother's eventual screaming couldn't wake him.

Then came lots of tears and people in uniforms. Everyone cried. They had to go to a small building and look at Father, sleeping in a coffin.

Sally was sure it wasn't him. She felt certain the softly spoken people who placed him in the coffin had made a doll of him instead, with waxy skin and coldness, maybe glass eyes too.

Sally thinks of all her memories as she tries to count the eyes around her. She gets to fifteen and then forgets what comes next.

Downstairs, more laughter.

Sally thinks about telling her mum about the time John asked her to sit on his knee.

She didn't want to, even though he promised her a packet of her favorite sweets.

When she did walk over, when she gave in, he put his hand on her leg and moaned. The same noise a person makes when they taste nice ice cream.

Sally cried. John laughed.

He is mean and horrible and his breath smells like the food they give their old cat, Bert.

John used to be her father's friend. Sally remembers, she remembers everything.

She remembers which eyes she hates the most, the eyes of the doll in the white dress. She has eyes the color of grass.

Sally doesn't like that.

She tried to sleep and block out the noise. She decides she needs to use the bathroom.

She worries a lot that she might bump into John because he sleeps in her mother's bed sometimes. Sally knows that because she saw him, and she can hear his awful pig snores.

She climbs from her small bed and takes Bessie the doll with her. Each set of eyes around the room follow her every move.

"Stop watching me," Sally whispers. It's no use, they never listen. Although they have ears, Sally checked.

She opens her door, creeps along the short landing, and into the bathroom. She wants a drink of water, but she doesn't dare to ask.

Sometimes, her mother shouts at her. Instead of getting upset, Sally feels as if she might be boiling inside, boiling like the saucepans do when her mother cooks.

She leaves the bathroom as stealthily as she can. She freezes as she hears a creak on the stairs. She knows which stair it is, step number seven.

John appears.

"Hello, Sally," he leers.

"Night," she mumbles.

"Hold on, do you want me to tuck you in?"

John's voice is slurring. Sally doesn't know why. "No," she says. She decides that if he tries to come near her, she will scream until her mother comes. She knows she will do something, even though she looks at her differently since Father fell asleep in the garden forever.

"Awww, don't be like that, little lady. I'm going to be your new daddy. How about that?"

His eyes are blue. Crafty, vile eyes. Wide ones, nosey ones. Wretched and awful.

Sally doesn't want a new father. She wishes John were dead.

She said that once, and her mother slapped her hard across the face. Still, she can think it, no one can tell.

With Bessie by her side, Sally feels stronger. John stands at the top of the stairs and wobbles.

"Push him," a barely there voice says.

She doesn't. She goes into her bedroom and closes the door.

Sally would rather be looked at by the doll's eyes than John's.

"Kill him," Bessie tells her.

"Shhhhh," Sally warns. No one can know Bessie is alive, no one can know she speaks, even though her mouth doesn't open. She came alive the day after her father went to sleep.

Her mother said he went to sleep forever. Sally knows that isn't true because even sleeping beauty woke up after a hundred years.

She climbs back into bed, with a hand placed firmly over Bessie's mouth.

"We're safe," she tells her doll. "All safe."

Sally watches the multiple dolls watch her. She wonders if they are planning something terrible. She worries that, if she falls asleep, she might wake up to all these dolls climbing all over her, biting like rats do.

"Kill John," Bessie says as soon as her mouth is free.

"Be quiet," she warns.

Her body turns cold as her door handle gets turned. She squeezes her eyes shut tightly and prays for her father to wake up so he can rescue her.

"Sally," comes the sound of John's scratchy voice. He sings her name, and the noise makes her brain itch.

He steps into her room slowly. Just one step.

Sally holds her breath, she grips Bessie tight as a tear slips down her face.

"John!"

She hears the voice of her mother. Her heart soars in relief. The door shuts with a click.

"Kill him," Bessie repeats.

"Yes, okay," Sally answers.

It isn't hard for her to stay awake with all those eyes watching her. Sally waits for the sound of her mother and John going to bed.

She takes hold of Bessie firmly and carries her downstairs.

"What shall we do?" Sally asks.

Now Bessie has that *look*, the look where words aren't needed. But her eyes hold a sparkle of mischief, a glint of revenge.

Bessie lifts her stuffed arm and points to the box of matches.

Sally knows she isn't allowed to go near them. Mustn't go near them. Still, she hitches up her long nightdress and reaches for the box.

She knows how to make fire with each match, has seen her mother do it a hundred times.

She strikes one sharply and watches the flame burn. She sees the orange light reflected in Bessie's eyes. She likes the pretty color. She blows it out, just like when she has birthday candles and lights another.

She throws it on the old sofa, lights another, and repeats. Tendrils of smoke begin to rise. Sally feels a bubbly of joy. John won't want to move in when they don't have a house to live in. She starts to laugh wildly. She lights more matches and places them on the soft fluffy cushions.

She coughs, the smoke starts to hurt her chest.

"Get outside," Bessie whispers. There is an urgency to her tone.

Sally does as she is told, pays attention. She can't reach the catch on the front door, so she goes to the back one and flings it open. She lets the old cat Bert out too, watches him flee into the night. She likes Bert's eyes.

The fresh air feels nice. She runs to the front garden to watch. She feels excited, like the time she went to a firework display and gazed at the roaring hot bonfire.

By the time neighbors come streaming out of their houses, by the time loud fire engines come blazing down the street, the house is the biggest bonfire she could ever have imagined.

Flames lick and consume every inch with wanton glee. Thick black smoke fills the sky. Sally wonders if it might reach the moon.

A blanket gets wrapped around her, she gets lifted up in the air and pulled away.

"Is anyone inside?" A lady shouts.

Sally doesn't like her wild eyes, so she cries until the woman leaves. The elderly woman from down the street, the one with all the cats, comes to hold her hands.

"I'll keep you safe," she says.

Her eyes are different. One is almost white, the other a glassy blue. Sally decides she likes her.

"Stay with her," Bessie whispers.

So, Sally does. She stays with the nice lady with the odd eyes. Together they watch massive hosepipes put the inferno out. Until her grandmother arrives with her red, wet, and sore eyes.

"What happened Sally?" Her grandmother wails. A man in a uniform stands with her. He watches her like her dolls did.

Sally forgets about the matches, she thinks of all the glass eyes burning until they vanish into ash piles. She almost smiles.

"Say, John did it," Bessie hisses quietly.

"John. It was John who did it, Grandmother," Sally repeats. "He played with matches. I saw him. He had a grown-up drink and shouted. Me and Bessie the doll ran."

It is then that Sally decides eyes are actually extremely useful. With a keen pair of eyes, you can lie about what you saw, and no one will ever know. A brain might record it, but no one can check or play it back to see.

"Are you sure?" The uniformed man asks. "You saw him?"

"I saw him with my own eyes," Sally lies. "He did it on porpoise."

"She means on purpose," her grandmother clarifies.

"Who was inside?" The uniform man asks. "They found two bodies."

He tries to say that last line quietly and fails. Sally hears and answers him.

"Mother was," she says. At this, her grandmother gasps and wobbles. "My dolls and John. Bert the cat ran away."

"Sorry for your loss," the man says.

Sally doesn't understand. What loss? Bert is fine, and she hated John. She hated the dolls, she hated her mother's eyes too. Her mother tried to replace her father, she could see the guilt and selfishness in her windows to the soul. Her mother blamed her for letting Father go to sleep, blamed her with cold, narrowed eyes.

"Come on, child, I'll look after you. I'll keep you safe," her grandmother sobs.

Sally looks at Bessie.

For the first time in her stuffed life, the doll smiles and winks.

VOYEUR

Are you alone?

Are you quite certain?

It might be best that you check. I like to watch people. People just like you.

I like to gaze upon a person's mannerisms, facial expressions, and habits. You wouldn't believe the things I get to see, the things people do when they think no one is looking. It gives me a kind of sexual thrill, a euphoric high. Watching others leaves me with a delicious, rich taste in my mouth and a desire for more.

People can be fascinating.

The lone man in the small cafe trying to catch the pretty woman's eye and failing, disappointment landing in his posture. The group of three friends, one slowly being pushed out, ignored, and rejected. The elderly man, making his way along a street, the way he stops to stare around him. What must he be thinking?

The tall man in the queue, checking his phone constantly, sighing, waiting, hoping for news.

In a world where every person seems in a frantic rush, I like to stop. I like to watch.

I see a thousand lives that aren't my own.

I know everyone's secrets, everyone's hopes and dreams, everyone's twisted perversions.

The French have a pretty word for those like me. Voyeur.

See how the letters roll off your tongue so smoothly, so naturally. Vowels and consonants forming two syllables of harmony.

The word makes my niche obsession sound innocent and exotic, harmless.

It did start that way.

Watching people doesn't give me an erection, I don't sit and play with myself if that's what you think. I'm not some dirty old man masturbating over young, lithe, and supple flesh.

The erection bit is kind of impossible anyway, considering I'm a woman.

Besides, Voyeurism is an art form. It's a craft, a skill.

And yes, I'm female and damn proud of it. I like dresses and the color pink. I like sharp knives and I am a voyeur, among other things.

I once saw a man masturbate over a crinkled photo of an old umbrella; he wore a thick oven glove on his busy hand. Each to their own, I guess. Really, I don't mock anyone for their life choices. I keep their secrets, treasure them all.

Lots of people have sex, in all different kinds of ways. Truthfully, that gets a little dull after a while, aside from the elderly sadist couple, that was interesting.

Another time, I saw a woman choke herself with her own pair of tights. She passed out for a short while but she was fine, she just kept on doing it. Once, I watched a man take handful after handful of pills. I didn't intervene. I mean, why would I? I wasn't supposed to know.

Uncle Joe reacted differently. He bolted up and raced off to the man's room with a bundle of towels clutched in his arms as an excuse. No one answered the door, and so he panicked and called the sheriff. The man lived.

Cameras.

That's how we did it. By we, I mean my uncle and me.

Before tiny hidden cameras became commonplace, my uncle crawled around in air vents to spy on his motel guests. Luckily, he was a slim guy, exceptionally crafty too.

I missed that generation, thankfully. The air vents made excellent hiding places for our cameras though.

I came to work for my uncle at age sixteen, being a school dropout and all. Not because I wasn't smart, but because I couldn't be bothered with the whole school brainwashing thing.

Attend class, learn what they tell you to learn, think how they want you to think, act how they want, and so on.

A place where there is punishment for not obeying, like the rest of the world. A sexist, racist, system in place and held securely. Anyone different becomes an instant target. Anyone who might be poor, clever, or wears the wrong shoes, wrong clothes, or has the wrong face is doomed.

In go frisky spring lambs, the school spits them up and chews them out as regular sheep, off to breed, pay a crippling mortgage and pay taxes. Pour money into our capitalist society.

I didn't belong in that world. I wanted no part of it. I didn't fit in, couldn't fit in. I wasn't accepted by anyone. I couldn't force myself to conform. No one made sense to me.

I wanted to learn about hunting, bloody historic battles, serial killers, anatomy, profiling techniques, forensics, and our law.

Laws, those rules the patriarchal system lay down in order to keep us in line.

My school was religious minded too. How I hated that. Conform to a set belief system or burn in Hell for eternity. Control by fear.

I began to study cults, from good old crazy Jim Jones to the lesser-known Emin. Whack jobs, but some were clever in their own way to con the needy and alone.

It seemed to me that mainstream religions were cults too, just larger and more organized, wealthy, and therefore accepted.

Crazy views, when you stop to think about it. Especially regarding the female of the species.

From the moment women are born, they are taught that they are lesser than men. Created as an afterthought and nothing more. Molded from a sliver of the first man's rib.

Made as company for Adam. They want women to lie on their backs and obey. Pop-out children and keep their mouths shut and their legs wide open.

I call bullshit.

The men in charge back then feared women. Tried to keep us from realizing our true strength. That's my theory, anyway. Strangely, no teachers at school ever wanted to hear my thoughts. Instead, they wanted me to have endless therapy, as if they expected me to be the next school shooter.

My parents, both devout, booted me out of the house when I refused. That didn't matter. They never wanted me anyway, never loved me, that much was clear from the beginning. I was not the child they wanted. Not the docile, rule-following, pleasant, doll-loving little girl they desired to have.

And so I ended up with Uncle Joe. The renegade daughter sent to live with the reclusive motel owner.

A shortcut to the eventual route I was always destined to take.

Uncle Joe had a small reception room with an office attached to his own home. Next door sat the motel. It didn't look creepy.

It was clean, well taken care of, and had a large pond and woodland area at the back. The office had a fake and clever, moveable wall. It was so convincing that, for months, I had no idea a small private room lay tucked behind.

That room had a collection of television screens. Four in total. Live feeds.

Joe was not ashamed to let me in on his secret. We had a kinship, me and him. Both of us were cut from the same cloth and he recognized that in me. Both of us darker than light inside.

The first night he let me watch the cameras, I was transfixed. Obsessed. Until then, I only ever sat in busy cafes wearing sunglasses to watch people more easily. The cameras offered a whole new glimpse into private delights behind closed doors.

We soon formed a pattern. I checked people into our eight roomed roadside motel. If I liked the look of someone, I gave them one of the keys to the special rooms. Key three, five, or eight.

We were never at full capacity or busy, so generally, everyone received a special room.

Joe would go around carrying out maintenance and cleaning. I manned, or rather, *womaned* the desk. In the evenings, we would eat and settle in the secret room in silence.

For three years or so, I loved our little slice of the world. I knew I had finally found my niche, my muse in life. I felt it. Until the lonely guy died. His death triggered an awakening. The real me underneath my flesh woke up.

Joe had been around the back of the building tending to his pond. He enjoyed summer nights out there, with a chair and a beer, watching his big special fish swim in the cool water.

I envied the fact he had outside interests, but I liked my time alone with the screens, too.

That night, I watched a guy die very suddenly.

He wasn't doing anything much, just lying on his bed by himself, enjoying the free television channels, minding his own business.

I'd checked him in hours before. He was quiet, lonely, and a little uncomfortable in his own skin. I understood that feeling. I recognized it.

He made me feel curious, I put him in room five and stared at the live feed.

What kept me watching was his right foot. It kept twitching.

Almost as if the guy wasn't even aware of it. It fascinated me. Every five seconds, twitch, twitch, twitch.

I wanted to peer inside his brain and find out which part of his mind was responsible for the habit. What would happen if I poked his cerebellum? What body part might jerk or twitch if I did that?

The guy abruptly stood, staggered a few steps, and clutched his chest.

Oh! I thought. A heart attack. Interesting.

I settled back in my comfy chair to watch. His death looked more like he suffered an electric shock first, he danced wildly to music only he could hear before he dropped like a stone to the cheap carpet. His eyes stayed open, so I zoomed in to watch that essential light take an exit.

I couldn't take my eyes away from him. I hadn't seen anyone die before, and it was beautiful. So wonderfully unexpected.

I left him for half an hour before I sneaked across to the motel, down the hallway with my master keys, and into his room.

I only wanted to touch him. I only wanted to feel his skin. I swear it.

I closed the door behind me and stood over him.

What was his name? Oh yes, Gary Kline, traveling for a meeting. Poor old Gary.

Everything that made him, him, was gone, missing entirely.

I saw no white-lit tunnel open up for the guy, but maybe that was only for him to see. Still, I doubted it.

I crouched down beside him. A thin trickle of blood dripped from his nose.

"Gary. Mr. Gary Kline?" I said as if I expected to find several different Garys I might have to distinguish from.

Nothing. Sightless eyes no longer seeing. Hearing gone, heart failed and stopped.

Tick tock, Gary's time was up.

Dead in a cheap motel room, on a cheap carpet, on a route hardly anyone drove. All alone.

I placed my hand on his cheek. He didn't flinch like everyone else did if I ever tried to touch them. He didn't refuse my hand, didn't push me away.

The lifelessness of his skin made me gasp in pleasure. That waxy feel, the growing chill. It felt delicious. He lay face up, as if he decided to take a quick nap.

My hand found itself all over his chest, all over his body.

The feeling was exquisite.

Carefully, I lay down next to him and wrapped an arm firmly around his waist, I draped one leg over his two. It was the most comfortable I ever felt in my entire life. There was no judgment from him, no narrowed eyes, no stares of lust or hatred.

Just pure bliss. Serenity. Finally, I felt true acceptance.

By the time I forced myself to leave him, walk back down the hallway, and into our office, Uncle Joe was waiting. He was early to arrive back inside. The camera was still on, and he'd seen everything.

"It was just nice!" I argued. "There was no harm at all. I was just curious."

"It's necrophilia!"

"No, Joe. That means having sex with the dead. I think you saw we didn't do that."

"This is a step too far, it's abnormal."

"Oh, so wiring up hidden cameras so we can watch people *is* absolutely normal?"

Uncle Joe cracked open a beer and gazed at me in that way I hated. That look made me want to spit fire and boil inside. Everyone looked at me that way, except, it seemed, for the dead.

"I want to be me. I want to be free to be myself. What do you want me to do, Joe? Play with fucking dolls and knit shit?"

"Knit shit," Joe sniggered. "Knit shit!"

The atmosphere began to melt. Joe roared with laughter. I joined in because that's what a person is supposed to do. I knew that.

"Don't do it again," he warned. "I mean it."

"Okay," I agreed. "I won't."

But of course, I did.

More people die in cheap roadside motels than you might think. The next one to shuffle off the mortal coil was Joe himself.

The reaper came for him at one in the afternoon, and Joe didn't even get to finish his bacon sandwich.

I found him, face down, tucked in behind the reception desk. Only a single booted foot jutted out. The sight gave me a clue as soon as I walked in.

"Oh, shit," I said.

I did the right thing and called the sheriff.

"I'll be twenty minutes, don't touch him," he said in that *I don't like you, but I tolerate you,* tone of his. The same tone everyone reserved, especially for me.

I allowed myself ten minutes.

I locked the door and squeezed in next to dead Uncle Joe. I stroked his cheek and arms, his back and head, with all the attention of a lover. He was still warm. He cooled just a little as I had my hands on him.

I felt delirious with bliss. Uncle Joe had tried to love me. Tried hard, in fact. Something about me bothered him and bothered everyone who met me. A sense warned them to avoid me. I was a reverse magnet somehow. I knew that.

Still, I never knew why they should all feel that way.

I looked average.

Long brown hair down to my shoulders, hair I always wore in a ponytail and barely brushed. Plainclothes, I favored checked shirts and jeans, leather boots, and belts or plain dresses. I smiled when I needed to, I laughed when I was supposed to. I did everything everyone else did but without the success.

People gave me a wide berth and Joe had been one of them. Yes, he welcomed me and let me in on his secret, but had he trusted me? No. Had he loved me? No.

In that sense, he was just like my parents. Judgmental and hypocritical, cold and suspicious. Always shouting at me for having an opinion that didn't match their own.

I moved reluctantly and unlocked the door. I wet tissues and rubbed my eyes until they were red and wet.

I wore my most solemn expression when the sheriff pulled up. He climbed out of the car in that way of his that portrayed his fake superiority. He hitched his trousers up and tipped his hat.

"Who found him?" He bellowed as soon as he stepped in.

Our sheriff was no genius. That was obvious. Me, of course, I found him. We had no cars in the vacant lot, no rooms were taken. He knew I was the only one that could have stumbled across poor dead Joe.

"I did, he was just lying there, Sheriff. I'm very sad."

The medical examiner was called. When he arrived, I heard him suggest Joe might have died from an aneurysm. The sheriff looked disappointed I hadn't shot him dead myself.

Without ceremony, they took him away in a long bag.

"What happens now? What do I do?"

"Check all your paperwork, call your folks, let 'em know. Oh, and there'll be an autopsy. So, don't leave town."

He winked, tipped his stupid hat, and left.

I knew about autopsies. I read about them in great detail. I was a little envious of the people who got to root around in dead bodies for a living, exploring and getting to work out which bit did what and why.

Still, I guessed the judgy sheriff suspected I killed my own Uncle Joe, and he'd gone and made the assumption that the motel had been left to me.

Uncle Joe had indeed left instructions for me to take over the running of the motel in his absence or death. He told me all about it, but I didn't kill him, I swear.

Joe's death, however, was more convenient for the lifestyle I wanted. Besides, he was so old that it didn't matter so much, and he had started to become a liability.

He wanted to restrict my watching time, my camera time. He even went as far as to make us both a little schedule.

"You're young," he'd said. "You should be out enjoying life."

He couldn't understand that watching people *was* my entire life, as much as it was his or more. His death freed me in a way. I could evolve.

I didn't call my parents.

Later that day, a couple arrived, looking for a room. I liked the look of them both. She was tall and graceful, he was athletic and smiley. I gave them a room with a hidden camera and got on with the cleaning.

The day passed quickly with all the chores I found myself with. In the evening, I settled behind our hidden wall to watch.

The couple. They were sat against the bed's headboard, side by side, watching television. The guy was picking at his nails, the woman ate candy. Both stared at the television screen with glazed eyes, hypnotized.

Every so often, the guy would reach down and scratch his balls. I was just getting bored when the bell outside the office rang.

We didn't have many people come looking for a room late at night unless it was the married ones from town arriving to conduct affairs.

I checked the time, only nine. I shuffled the wall back across and opened the door.

"Evening," a tall man greeted me. "I was expecting some Norman Bates type to open the door. Can I have a room, please?"

He looked beautiful. Blue eyes and brown luscious hair. Tall and lithe. Suntanned too. On his back, he carried a huge backpack.

"Yes, come in," I said.

Damn shame there aren't cameras in the showers.

I immediately dug out key three.

"Do you accept cash? I have I.D," he said.

I waved an arm in his direction, "Cash is fine, don't worry about the I.D. We aren't too formal here."

We? I mean me. This place is all mine now. Nor bad for a school dropout.

He seemed happy with the arrangement and started talking. "I'm traveling across the states. I usually camp out, only, I need a bed for the night. My back hurts."

"Do you have a car?"

"No, I hitchhike. Do you know if there's any work around here?"

"Wow," I said. "That must be amazing. Are you sure it's safe? And I'm not sure, I'll make inquiries for you."

Safer for a man to travel, women can't go anywhere without having to worry. Wait, what if...

"There might be some work here, painting and maintenance," I said. I stepped towards him and tried to smile in a friendly way. The idea of having him around made my stomach feel warm.

"Here? You mean, here with you?" He asked.

"Yes."

I watched his face turn to disgust, apprehension, revulsion.

"Thanks, but I just remembered I have work lined up in another town soon. So…"

Liar.

"Okay, no problem," I said. My heart, the organ that had been pierced by rejection a thousand times before, felt an invisible dagger plunge in once more.

I handed him the key and grinned. Instead of smiling at me, or talking more, he frowned and stepped back.

"Well, I really need to sleep," he said. He stepped around me, placed money on the counter, and walked out. I went straight to our cameras, my cameras.

I watched him dump his backpack on the freshly cleaned carpet. I watched him unzip his jacket and check the sheets on the bed were clean. He sat and took off his boots, his shirt, his jeans and discarded them on the floor.

Hmmm. No underwear.

He stretched and walked into the bathroom.

The Norman Bates comment had given me an idea. Although I won't deny it had crossed my mind a thousand times before already. I followed the thread in my head. Once it unraveled, I found I couldn't help but chase it until I found the end.

Uncle Joe had left behind a cabinet full of pills. He hadn't been the healthiest of men. I dug around until I found a bottle of heavy sedatives, the ones he took for insomnia. I crushed four up together and poured them into a bowl of hot chicken soup and covered the taste with salt. I buttered fresh rolls and made a sandwich. I carried them all on a tray to the man's room and knocked.

"Oh," he said. He answered the door wrapped in a towel. "Is this for me?"

"Yes, I thought you might be hungry. No charge."

"That's so kind of you! Really! Thank you. I'm glad I found this place."

"Me too," I said. "We try hard for our guests. It's that kind of motel."

He took the tray and closed the door. I heard him lock it behind him.

He doesn't like me. Why doesn't anyone ever like me?

Was it my looks? My hair? My eyes? Did I smell bad?

My parents used to say I had dead eyes.

I shrugged and fled back to my secret room. The guy ate everything, fast. I sat chuckling like an evil bond villain and waited.

The couple was *still* watching television. They had to rank as the dullest pair I'd seen in a while.

By eleven I was feeling itchy. It felt as if little spikes of electricity were jumping all over my skin. My guy was asleep. Out cold. Only a single lamp lit up the room. He lay with his mouth open and one arm stretched out over his head.

I grabbed what I knew I was going to need from the kitchen, took the master key, and left.

It seemed as if the guy was a gift, just for me.

We didn't get a lot of backpackers passing through, and for one to arrive on the day Joe died appeared to be fate. I crept across to the motel, across the hallway, and opened his door.

The only sounds were his slight snores, little gentle puffs of air as his chest rose and fell. I didn't waste any time. I couldn't risk loud noises, not with other guests around. I tiptoed towards him, slowly, carefully.

I watched him. I watched his eyes flicker under his closed lids, dreaming. I saw drool drip from the corner of his mouth onto the cheap pillow.

I wondered about his thoughts, his ambitions, his life, and his family.

I raised my knife, the sharpest one we had, and plunged it straight into his chest. The thick metal went in easier than I expected.

His eyes flew wide open. He gasped, but no air went in or out. Absolute shock and horror. Those beautiful blue eyes blinked rapidly and landed on me. He snarled and buckled. It took less than a minute for him to fall still.

Now you won't leave.

I took my own clothes off and climbed into the bed next to him. Warm blood pooled underneath him, but I didn't mind. My own skin touched his as he cooled slightly. I moved his arm while it was still flexible, wrapped it around me, and curled up underneath it.

Glorious. It felt gloriously perfect. Peace settled inside me.

I stroked his chest, his face, his legs. Ironic that only the dead let me near them.

Within hours rigor mortis set in. Still, I stayed with him. Temporarily accepted and complete. Not once did he push me away. I was loved.

Eventually, at around five in the morning, I got up, showered, and bleached the bathroom. I wrapped his body in a plastic sheet and dragged him along the hallway. That was far tougher than I expected, nerve-wracking, too. I stored him around the back of the building while I cleaned his room. I knew I needed to replace the mattress, the carpet too. Until then, I wouldn't let the room out. I collected his things and threw them into the furnace in the cellar.

At the back of the motel sits Joe's little garden with his large pond. By large, I mean, twenty feet by fifteen or so. It was quite deep, with fish in and lily pads covering the surface.

I put rocks in with the body, wrapped a second sheet around, and bound the whole lot up with thick tape.

I wanted to keep the body. I wanted to keep it until it rotted and maggots found a home. It broke my heart to know I couldn't. So off he went into Uncle Joe's pond with barely a splash.

Once he sank down, he wasn't one bit visible. Lily pads closed over him, which felt quite poetic if you like that kind of thing.

I returned to my cameras. The couple was asleep, facing away from each other.

Yep, definitely the most boring guests.

I hadn't missed a thing.

I carried on as normal for quite some time. On occasion, a mean voice hidden away in my mind reminded me I was a killer.

Sometimes, I would be cleaning, or washing, minding my own business, and then the voice would start, a cold jolt would burst inside of me. Sweat would run down my back until my clothing felt shrink-wrapped.

In moments like that, I felt ashamed of myself. Truly and deeply. What right did I have to take a life? None.

I tried to see the man, the traveling hitchhiker man, my first, as a onetime opportunity. I admit, his life meant nothing to me. In death, he became valuable beyond words. The memory of our night together gave me a high for almost three months. Within that time, I organized Uncle Joe's funeral. I *did* make a curt phone call to my parents. They chose not to travel down to say goodbye to Joe. The church was their priority, not sinners like me and my dead Uncle.

I had the front of the motel painted cream. I ordered a new mattress and a new carpet.

I settled into my routine.

Every night, I would watch my guests. Couples, single guests, rare families.

Loneliness crept over me. Slowly at first, until it hit me hard.

I would find myself touching the people on my screens with my fingertips, craving the life they had inside themselves, yearning to be part of their world.

In the mornings, people would check out. They couldn't get away from me fast enough. The more I tried, the more they sensed my desperation.

Sadness took a firm hold. Until she walked in.

It was a bright Sunday afternoon. I was sitting in my seat at reception, building a tower out of playing cards. The door swung open and in she came.

The world tipped sideways.

She wore a summer dress, a yellow one with pretty flowers decorating the hem. She carried a leather bag and had sun-bleached, blonde hair that carried the scent of the ocean somehow. Her skin was smooth, unblemished, so different from my own. She had a way about her, a quality, a magnetic pull.

"Can I have a room, please?"

Her words were the same ones that everyone used, yet they were brand new the moment she spoke them. I stared at her, numb.

"Yes," I managed to say.

"Thanks, how much?"

I wanted to tell her it was free for her, anything would be free for her. Instead, I pointed at the sign I had.

"Okay, that's cool. Just for one night, please."

"Are you going anywhere nice?" I said and immediately felt stupid.

"Yes! A music festival. I'm meeting friends."

Friends. I was willing to bet she had hundreds. Not like me, who had none.

She was everything I wanted to be and couldn't. She brought sunshine into the office, confidence, and grace. My opposites.

I imagined that every time she spoke, people stopped to listen. Not like me. Whenever I spoke, people became offended.

I gave her room key three.

"Are you hungry?" I said. "I can make you some chicken soup? Later I mean."

"Sorry, I'm a vegetarian."

Of course she is.

She took the key and rummaged in her bag for her money. As soon as she placed the cash on the counter, she backed away, frowning.

"Have a nice stay," I mumbled. She nodded and closed the door behind her. The room immediately turned cold.

I watched her with greedy eyes all afternoon.

I hung a sign on the office door, telling people to ring the bell. I bolted the door and sat in my secret room.

She unpacked her small bag and took a shower. She wore a long yellow t-shirt and plain underwear.

She lay down and slept. Her wet hair spread out behind her. She placed her hands together as she dozed, as if she were praying.

Temptation twisted around inside me.

I can't. She has a car. I can't dump that in the pond. Or could I dump it at the scrap yard? The lake? No. Stop.

Her small car sat parked up outside the motel. I wondered if she was planning on picking her friends up. Tanned and beautiful girls all crammed together in a car. I couldn't imagine what that might feel like, to be one of them, fun and carefree.

People like that look down on me. It comes naturally to them. They automatically view me as being far below them. Girls like her would never choose or want me as a friend.

I zoomed in on her sleeping face, the curve of her shoulder, the arch of her back. All that smooth, warm flesh. Flesh that would never touch mine.

I turned the screen off. Slid my fake wall across and went to make organic vegetable soup.

"This is amazing of you! Are you sure I can't pay you?"

"It's fine, don't worry. I like our guests to be happy," I told her. "It's that kind of motel."

She looked sleepy when I knocked on her door. She brightened as soon as she saw the tray. One big bowl of vegetable soup with five sedatives mixed in, three fresh rolls, a beer, and a candy bar.

"Thank you."

I smiled and left. Back down the hallway and across to the office, straight to my cameras.

She put the television on and watched the news while she ate.

She was quite thin, too thin. I used too many sedatives. Twenty minutes after she finished eating, she started fanning herself. Sweat began forming on her skin. She stood up to use the bathroom and fell back down heavily. She curled herself into a ball and groaned.

I wondered if she knew then, or suspected. Or maybe she thought she had food poisoning.

Her phone sat on the bedside table, one of those new expensive ones. She tried to make a grab for it and dropped it instead.

Her hand flopped back down onto the mattress and bounced. I waited for five minutes, ten minutes, twenty minutes before I took the master key and left.

She appeared to be sleeping heavily when I opened the door. It was dark outside, but a lamp was on. I crept close to the bed on tiptoes.

I touched her leg, a small stroke across her bare thigh. She didn't flinch. For a second, I wondered if she was already dead. Then I saw the soft rise and fall of her chest. I crossed to the other side of the room and picked up a pillow.

I shouldn't do this. Just leave, she might never know I drugged her. Just leave, now.

I took a deep breath and shuddered.

I slammed the pillow down on her face.

Her reflexes kicked in seconds later. I had to climb across her and hold the pillow down. She was thrashing so wildly. Her whole body buckled underneath me. Her hands flew up and scratched my arms deeply. I tried to count how long it took, but I couldn't keep track. She fell still. I kept the pillow pressed down for another sixty seconds.

No heartbeat. No breath. No life.

I liked knives the best, but the mess was too much.

I took her t-shirt off and brushed her soft hair.

I stripped off my own clothes and lay next to her. I kissed her blue lips, a soft kiss, and held her tight.

I told her all about my life, whispered secrets into her lifeless ears. No resistance. She let me hold her. Let me touch her. We became the best of friends and no one disturbed us all night. No new guests, no one.

Close to morning, I smashed her phone up. I flushed its sim card down the toilet. I carried her things to the furnace and burned them. Her, I left in bed.

"I'll be back later," I told her.

I drove her car to the lake three miles away and watched it plummet from the edge to the bottom. A gift for the water. I walked back, a happy bounce in my step.

I got on with my day.

When I returned that night, she was stiff and cold. Her skin was changing color. The room smelt rotten.

I didn't want her to leave me. Not so soon. Even the thought made me sad inside. I knew there would never be another like her.

Her chilled skin welcomed me once more. Eventually, I fell asleep next to her.

In the middle of the night. She went to her grave in Joe's pond. My tears added to the churned water.

So that was then, and this is now.

I watch every guest. Every night.

Every so often, one catches my eye.

Four months after my woman, a lone man arrived. He wasn't much to look at, but he too had a way about him I liked. He was on his way to a job interview, one he hoped to get but never arrived at. He liked chicken soup too.

We spent two nights together, me and him. Two wonderful nights.

There are currently three bodies in Joe's pond. Two men, and one extraordinary woman. I know I'll be caught one day.

My woman was reported missing from this area. The meddling sheriff came to my motel. He asked me his moronic questions. I showed him the register. The woman, my beautiful woman, hadn't signed in. I told him I hadn't seen her or her car.

"Mighty strange," he said. "She was heading here by all accounts."

"Not really strange," I smiled. "People change their minds all the time."

I should stop, I know I should. Yet, I can't. I have a compulsion. A need. One that's hard to feed in this modern day.

It's not enough to watch people anymore, not enough to observe and wonder. Not enough to peer into lives and habits.

Uncle Joe stayed content as a Voyeur his entire life. I suppose many others do too.

I evolved.

Sometimes I think I watch others the way a lion watches a gazelle before they decide to pounce. I always had a hunger bubbling away under the surface. I always wanted more. I prefer the dead to the living. The dead prefer me, the living hate me on sight.

I need to feel dead flesh against my living skin.

I need to watch the spark of life fade away. I need death pressed close. I want to be loved and accepted.

There is a short blonde woman in room five.

I'm watching her right now. She is on her phone, in the middle of a heated argument by the looks of things. She is heartbroken or sad, upset, and worried. She twists her wedding ring around her finger and cries. Sometimes she shouts loudly.

Would she still swear and yell if she knew I was watching her? Would she still grasp her hair and yank it in frustration? Would she still cry so messily?

Does she know she might die tonight?

Perhaps I will make her a bowl of homemade chicken soup, you know, just to cheer her up a little.

It really is that kind of motel.

A DISCOVERY OF TUNNELS AND TIME

When I was six years old, in nineteen eighty-four, Nina moved in next door.

I watched excitedly from the window as a moving van and car pulled up. She climbed out the back of the car, tightly clutching a doll just like my own. She wore a pink dress and had a red ribbon I instantly wanted, tied in her pretty hair.

I jumped up and down on our old couch until Ma yelled at me to quit.

I felt so happy, I knew then we were destined to be the very best of friends.

We seemed to be the same age, and it was fate. I wanted to meet her straight away.

Ma said it wasn't polite to disturb the family on their first day in a new house, so I sat and daydreamed about our future adventures together instead.

In my mind I saw us playing in the treehouse in our garden. I saw us growing up and working in a fancy office like the smart ladies on television did.

I imagined we'd share a house, a pink one, and fill it with dolls and fluffy cushions, sweets, ice cream, and chocolate milk.

My sense was right, kind of.

We did make friends, and we quickly grew to be inseparable. By the age of ten, we were sleeping at each other's houses every weekend. She could finish my sentence, and I could finish hers. We would marvel over our differences in skin color, be envious of each other's hair, wear each other's clothes and call each other's parents Ma two and Pa two. Nina and Jane, Jane and Nina, our names fitted together perfectly.

Our families called us twins, not of body but twins in spirit, and we loved that.

At age fifteen, just after Nina's birthday, which was close to my own, we found the tunnel.

We often wandered the woodland behind our houses. We made each other daisy chain crowns and declared ourselves to be queens of the land. There was a pond that always smelt rancid, plenty of lush, thick trees and further back, the bad area which had the sewer entrance. We were forbidden to go that way or venture that far, but we were growing up, rebelling.

One ordinary Saturday, I fled my house after an argument with Ma. I wanted to start wearing make-up, Ma had forbidden it. I had a tube of bright red lipstick I was very proud to own.

"That color belongs in the bin, not on your face!" Ma wailed and threw it away.

I stomped out to the woods to wait for Nina.

She must have heard the blazing row, she soon came out and found me waiting.

"I wish we could just run away and leave this horrible place," I whined as soon as I saw her.

"Don't be dramatic," she laughed. "We're lucky. Come on, let's go for a walk."

Nina was always the wisest one of us, the smartest and the bravest too. I was the ungrateful, pouting, forever complaining sidekick.

We walked arm in arm like we always did. We took the path we'd chosen a thousand times, winding past trees, past the stinking pond.

"I want to see the sewers. I heard my pa say a body was found there, just last week," Nina announced.

"What body?" I shrieked. "A dead one!"

"Yes, a dead one! And I don't know. Just someone, I guess. A stranger maybe. It's all very hush, hush."

Nina's Pa was one of the few police officers in our small town. That generally meant she overheard all the juiciest pieces of gossip and knew about all the small crimes.

"Who found the body?" I asked.

"I don't know, I heard Ma and Pa talking. I wished we would have found it."

"Yuk," I said.

I hadn't had any run-ins with death by then. Everyone I knew and cared about was still alive. Dying seemed an impossible far-off concept, like marriage and children, taxes, high-heeled shoes, and college.

"You're being mordid," I said.

"It's pronounced morbid Jane, and no I'm not, I'm just curious."

Nina wanted to grow up and become a scientist. She had firm dreams, unlike me. I figured I might have to be a scientist too, so I could study with her and work in the same place, doing complicated science stuff.

Nina ruffled my hair and took off running.

"Wait for me!" I yelled.

I would have followed and chased her to the ends of the earth and so, of course, off I went after her.

We stopped at a slight grassy slope. Facing us was a running stream, surprisingly clear water glittered in the bright sun. After that stood a layer of thick trees, standing in a line, soldier-like.

"Look at that, it's huge!" Nina pointed.

I followed her gaze and my eyes landed on a fat sewer pipe, as big as us. Bigger, in fact. It seemed remarkably clean. It looked more like a tunnel. A strip of yellow crime scene tape flickered in the slight breeze.

"This must be where they found the body and it can't be a sewer!" I said. "It doesn't smell like poop."

"No, but you do," Nina giggled and elbowed me sharply in the ribs. She turned and ran, splashing across the water, and stood in front of the huge tunnel.

"HELLOOOO," she shouted. I caught up and listened to her voice echo and repeat itself.

"I'm going in," she said.

"What! Don't be crazy! You'll catch diseases and you'll stink. Ma will murder me if I go in there. It's worse than wearing red lipstick."

"It doesn't even have a grate! Aren't you curious to see where it goes?"

Yes, I was. Very curious. The bad area, the sewer, was off bounds to us, forbidden. Yet it didn't seem like such an awful place to me.

Still, the hairs on the back of my neck stood on end. My stomach started to hurt with worry. The thought of leaving the bright sunshine behind chilled me. I wondered if a murderer lurked in the darkness, waiting for girls like us. Goosebumps broke out over my skin.

My mind made the decision to step back, but Nina held out her hand.

Instinctively, I took it.

Our heads failed to touch the roof of the tunnel as we walked. There was plenty of room to move and the metal sphere was as dry as a bone.

"This is creepy," I muttered. "Wait, is that blood?!"

I pointed to the reddish-brown stain on the ground as my stomach lurched.

"No!" Nina laughed as we inched our way forward. We were leaving the sun behind, it started to get colder and dark.

"It's probably rust," she said and peered closer.

"There could be rats in here, big ones," I warned. "Or mutant turtles, like in the cartoon."

Nina rolled her eyes at me and pulled me along. For a while, the only sounds were our trainers slapping down onto the metal.

"What if…" I said.

"Hush Jane, look."

We faced a decision. Left or right. The tunnel split in two separate directions. To me, both felt wrong. I only wanted to go back the way we came.

Ma always said that sometimes, the fate of a person's life could be determined by which direction they chose to go. Go right and they get knocked down by a car, go left and they'll be safe and happy. A careless choice, a small choice, with vastly different outcomes to both.

Before I could complain or speak, Nina pulled us right. By my reckoning, we were walking underneath the actual woodland. The idea felt wrong and bizarre. The perfect sphere of the tunnel wasn't being warped or pushed out of shape by thick tree roots above.

"How did they hollow all this out?" I asked.

"I don't know, machines I guess."

We carried on walking in silence. I gripped Nina's hand tightly.

"Listen," she said. "I can hear birdsong."

I couldn't. I couldn't hear a single thing. Only the thudding of my own heartbeat sounded.

We both saw the glimmer of light at the same time, the slight suggestion of sunlight caught our eyes.

I bet we come out near town, I thought. Near the supermarket or near the park. Have we walked that far though?

Nina dashed ahead, I followed.

We found our exit, our way out. We found ourselves in a different world altogether.

At first, it seemed perfectly normal. No one was around and I felt glad for that. We pushed our way through heavy, spiky bushes and out into the sun.

Neither of us wanted to be caught strolling out of the sewer. We were in the park, the empty park.

"It's a big shortcut," Nina observed. She was right, and it made no sense. The walk to the park in town always took an hour or more.

"Where is everyone?" I said.

The park was usually clustered with people on a weekend. Our town was small, but every child longed to be on the swings and roundabouts or fighting over the seesaw.

"I don't know."

I felt around in my pocket for coins. I had enough pocket money left to buy us both a cold can of coke.

"Let's go to the shop," I said. It was my turn to pull her along. A curious feeling made me stop.

I felt unsettled, almost as if I were upside down or missing some essential part of myself. A wave of dizziness hit me.

"This doesn't feel right," I said.

"Jane, Jane with her head in the rain," Nina sang. "Chill out, it's all cool."

We walked across the grass and up to the main road. No cars were in sight. Not one. I glanced across the street and gasped. The small shop had boarded-up windows. Wooden planks covered every door and entry. The shop next door was the same, and the hairdressers looked as if a fire had occurred. Outside was all black and charred.

When did this happen? This isn't right.

I felt cold all over, that kind of deep cold that seeps into your bones. I started to shake and whimper.

"Nina, please. We need to go."

"It's fine! Something happened overnight, that's all," she said, although she didn't look convinced. She squeezed my hand firmer.

"Did your pa say anything?" I asked. If anyone knew something terrible had happened, it surely had to be him.

"No."

"Oh."

We gazed around. The silence felt far too loud. We stood with our mouths open, not really knowing what to do until we heard a piercing gut-wrenching scream. A high-pitched wail of fury that made us both jump.

Racing around the corner of the street came a person with ribbons of ripped clothing streaming out behind them. Nina and I froze, wide-eyed with terror.

It's a man! I could see his beard, a long tangled and stained beard.

He sprinted fast. He was covered head to toe in mud or grime, or something. He raised his arms and screeched, a terrifying banshee sound.

He's coming for us!

"RUN," I shouted and yanked my friend. In my struggle to pull her, she staggered backward and fell.

"UP!" I screamed, wild panic engulfed me. I felt bile burn in my chest and throat. I dragged my friend until the man was almost upon us.

Nina scrambled up. I lost my grip, and she ran for the park.

"The tunnel!" I yelled. "Nina, get to the tunnel!"

She was running the wrong way entirely. The wild man veered off and chased her.

What do I do? What do I do?

I jumped up and down on the spot, my mind and body wanted two different things.

I have to save Nina.

So many thoughts spiraled around in my mind. I thought of my parents at home and likely worried sick about me.

Are they safe? How long has the man been rampaging?

It made sense, it had to be why everyone was hiding indoors.

But where are the police? Are they too scared? But Nina!

My heart lurched, my feet pounded. I almost ran back to the tunnel before my brain took me the other way. I heard my best friend scream my name, and I sprinted to the sound.

Close to the child's swings, the wild man had her pinned down. He was trying to bite her while she kicked and lashed out furiously.

I didn't think. Not one bit. I ran at them. I rammed my shoulder straight into him and knocked him away from her. Nina lay choking and gasping, tears running down her face.

"What's wrong with you?!" I shouted at the stranger. "We did nothing to you!"

He was on all fours, winded. I swear I heard him growl, low and threatening. That sound conveyed a thousand terrible and horrifying promises.

"The bottle," Nina gasped.

"What?"

Nina pointed and sat up.

A shiny large, empty vodka bottle lay near the rubbish bin. For a moment, I was confused, wondering why she wanted it, and then I realized. I bolted for it, grabbed it by the neck, and brought it down hard on the man's skull.

I only wanted to stop him from getting up.

The bottle broke apart on impact. The vibration of the blow hurt my arm. Thick shards of glass went bouncing off. The man fell face down, still and quiet. Blood burst from his head in a thick stream.

"Nina, quick. We need to get the police," I cried. "I've bloody killed him!"

My teeth started to chatter.

She shook her head. "No, he's only knocked out. Listen, you were right. something's wrong here."

I helped her to her feet. I didn't dare let my eyes leave the body of that man. I expected him to climb to his feet, any moment, and come tearing after us, after me.

Nina read my mind. "Watch him," she said and crossed to the bin.

She began to root through it.

What is she doing? Our situation felt utterly surreal.

"We need to go," I hissed. "What are you doing in the bloody bin?"

"Looking for this," she said and held up a soggy newspaper with triumph.

Not one of the printed words made much sense to me. Some of the pages were torn, some were missing, some were too wet to read. Nina understood and broke it down for me.

Essentially, our local newspaper, our own town reporters, had written of a countrywide rage virus.

RG-1788GB to be exact. A terrible fast-spreading disease that caused people to behave differently. An infected person became violently angry and aggressive and was to be avoided at all costs. They said that chemicals in the brain altered dramatically, very suddenly. I hadn't even known the brain had chemicals in it. Scientists were working hard on a cure. The military had been overpowered in some places.

"Jane, oh my God, listen to this! Leading experts are currently involved in research into infected water samples from ground zero. Ground zero is here!"

The virus had started in our town. Our small slice of the world had become famous for all the wrong reasons. Quarantines had failed, most of the infected had breached blockades in a mass riot. Many people were dead.

"Wait, they wrote this and printed it, so it means they're alive still. Where are the newspaper offices? We could get there."

"Hold on," I said. "This can't be real. There was nothing on the news or radio. Ma wouldn't let me out of the house if all this was going on."

Nina sat down heavily on a bench and stared around her.

I want to go home, I want to go home, I want to go home.

I wished I had two red shoes I could click together and instantly appear at home.

"This is so weird. We need to leave, not go off exploring Nina. All this is crazy. We would have heard. It's not true."

"My brother reads comics," Nina answered. "Sometimes I borrow them."

"Oh, I…"

"They have mad stories about alternative worlds."

"Huh?"

I sat down too then. I kept one eye on the man and another on the street. I wondered if the man was dead. I was no expert, but it looked to me as if he was.

I tried to consider Nina's idea, but it seemed too fantastical. A bit like the plots of the science fiction shows Pa watched. I doubted anyone could wander down a sewer tunnel and end up in an alternative world. I mean, surely that meant sewer workers would be popping off someplace else every five minutes.

"Take the paper. Let's go home and show our parents. Okay?" I said. "They'll know what to do. Pa two can call his police friends."

"Yeah, okay."

"Nina, I'm a murderer, that man is…"

An almighty boom sounded in the distance. I watched a giant fireball erupt and reach for the sky.

Is that the petrol station?

It seemed to come from that general direction. I certainly didn't want to go and look. I was sick of being in the weird version of our town. I wanted nothing more than to leave. Nina stood and held my hand. My heart soared with relief.

"Talk later," she hissed. "We gotta go."

A ring of bruises was beginning to form around her throat, and I noticed her limp.

"Hurt my knee," she said. I put my arm firmly around her.

Just get us home, tell Ma. No, tell all of our parents. They'll all know what to do. Wait, what if…

"I know! Maybe our town is a film set for the day?" I ventured. "Or it's an elbrate prank?"

"The word is elaborate," Nina said and shrugged. She jammed the newspaper in her back pocket.

We managed to get a few feet across the park before I heard them.

Growls and howls of fury. A static hiss started up in my mind, while my skin felt full of electricity. A whole gang, a big group, a pack, came barrelling up the street. At least twenty dirty, filthy people with one woman in the lead. A glint of metal caught the sun. A big knife gripped in the leader's hand.

A cold dread threatened to swallow me up.

"Nina," I whined.

"I know! RUN!"

I took her weight as much as I could bear. The crowd saw us and whooped with manic joy.

They came straight for us, coming faster than we could move.

They're going to tear us apart. Rip us limb from limb. They're going to kill us.

I lurched forward and vomited down myself. Tears stung my eyes.

"Quick, quick," I yelled.

Please, please, please. We can make it!

Nina, my wonderful Nina, my very best friend, stumbled and fell. Her knee gave way, and she went crashing to the cold grass face first.

NO, NO, NO.

My heart pounded. I screamed in terror.

"GET UP," I cried.

The crowd behind us shouted in triumph. They were too close. I reached out for Nina, and I let my hand fall.

No time. Go, GO!

She raised her head. Our eyes met, and she quickly understood I was going to abandon her. I saw the fear, the shock, and betrayal in her eyes. I knew in a single second that I had no chance to live if I stopped. The instinct to survive had me in its tight grip.

"I'm sorry," I said.

I turned and ran. My legs took me before my mind could catch up.

The crowd pounded towards her, I could feel the vibrations in the ground under my own feet. I craned my head as they jumped on her. In a hive-minded movement without mercy, they had her. Tearing and ripping her clothes and flesh. I forced my way through the bushes and back into the tunnel. I heard her screams of agony. I heard her crying out for me, screaming my name, begging for help.

I did not dare to look behind again.

For an hour or so, I sat on the cool metal and felt disgusted with myself. I screamed, I cried. I panicked. I couldn't find the courage inside myself to go back to that place, to go back for my Nina.

I left her behind. The crowd didn't even try to follow me into the darkness, they made no attempt to chase after me. We could have made it? I should have tried. I should have gone down fighting by her side.

My place was always by her side.

I had no idea of how I was going to explain anything. I had no idea of what I was going to say to our parents. Nina had the newspaper. I had no proof. I had nothing but shame.

Eventually, I climbed to my feet and followed the route back out. My head pounded, my heart kept skipping beats. When I finally reached the exit, it was dark outside.

Impossible, we were only gone for hours!

I made my way home like a condemned prisoner. One slow step at a time.

What if it was an alternative world? What if this one is too? What if I never get home?

I let myself in the back way, and in through the back door.

"Ma," I croaked. "I left her."

I braced myself to be shouted at and screamed at. Instead, Ma ran in and dropped to her knees. She sobbed and hugged me tightly.

Turned out, Nina and I had been missing for three days.

I tried hard to explain everything to Nina's parents. They shouted so much that my ears hurt. I tried hard to explain what happened to the police detectives. I asked them to search the tunnel, to go right and to take big guns and to be careful. I begged them to seal it, to shut it off.

Whenever I managed to sleep, I had dreams of the horde of infected people finding their way into our world and coming for us all. In my nightmares, Nina was one of them, coming for revenge, coming for me. I saw the face of the man I felt sure I killed over and over.

The police *did* search. They found nothing, only dead ends.

A kind detective talked about noxious gases, hallucinations, drugs, and fantasies. They sent a man in a smart suit to talk to me.

"What your version of events is… is impossible, Jane."

"It can't be impossible, because it's true," I answered.

"Tell us where Nina's body is. We'll understand and we'll help you."

I told him. I left her at the park when the horde came. I told him they might find pieces of her there, but only pieces. I told him I wasn't brave, told him I wasn't strong enough to have been able to save her.

He said I had concocted my wild story out of guilt.

I had to stay in my bedroom and swallow pills four times a day. My parents couldn't bear to look at me. The police came by every evening. They talked about sending me away, sending me to a place to heal my sick mind, a place that might discover the truth locked away inside my head.

No one believed me. No one.

I cried constantly. Heartbroken and angry with myself. I missed Nina terribly. The guilt ate away at my soul.

Around five days later, stuck in a limbo of misery, I heard sirens in our street.

They're coming for me. I'll be taken to prison any moment now.

Half of me felt glad to go. I deserved to be punished for leaving her.

I whimpered and hid under my covers. I waited for the firm knock at our door.

Instead, the police screeched to a halt three doors down. A man had killed his wife. My parents started arguing downstairs, vicious words thrown at each other.

An hour later, the police were back outside. A woman across the road had killed her teenage son.

Violence broke out all over our town.

Ma and Pa's argument raged on louder downstairs. They smashed things, swore, and screamed. I barricaded my door and cried until the house turned quiet.

"Ma?" I shouted as I crept out.

When I finally plucked up the courage to venture down. They were both dead. Both had terrible head injuries inflicted by each other.

I vomited, I screamed, I cried. I called the police; the line was busy. I ran out into the street, desperate for help.

People raced around, yelling and punching each other. Our quiet cul-de-sac had become a war zone. Our world had become the alternate one.

Fires burned in homes, no fire engines arrived to help.

What's happening? Why is this happening? Did the horde come for us all? Are they here?

Nina always joked that I was slow to pick up on ideas, but it was then that I realized.

We didn't go to another world; we went to the future. The virus, I brought it back. I'm patient zero. I did this. I infected everyone.

Knowledge flooded my system, and I wailed in despair. Screams and shouts came closer, closer. I ran back inside to think.

I wanted to wait in the park. I wanted to wait for myself and Nina to appear so I could see us, or rather them, back. The whole concept hurt my brain and I had no idea if I was right or not. I knew I likely had to wait a while for the newspaper we found to be printed.

Maybe, I can get through the tunnel and warn myself in the past? Or warn Nina? Can that even happen? Because it didn't happen, a version of me didn't appear that day.

The more I thought about it, the more my mind got into a ravel. Still, I had to try.

Helicopters sounded overhead, big double-bladed ones. Army trucks headed down the main roads. I knew it was all pointless, I saw the newspaper after all.

The virus was going to spread. The whole country was in trouble, so many would die because of me.

I felt sad about that, more than sad, heartbroken. But I wanted Nina back. I figured I had one chance to save her and by doing that, I could save everyone. I was going to undo the damage. I had to be strong, I had to be brave. I had to be more like Nina.

My plan was simple: I was going through the tunnel. I wanted to do a reset like Pa did with his videotapes and cassettes, record over events.

I took Ma's biggest shiny knife with me. I dressed in dark clothing and left the house.

On our street alone, four fires burned. Our elderly neighbor, Mrs. Prince, stood with a baseball bat in her hand, cackling wildly at a twitching, bloody body under her feet.

Ignore it all, don't look. I can fix it. It won't exist soon. It'll be like it all never even happened.

Mrs. Prince roared at me and started lurching forward after me. I ran.

I raced through our town, a war zone. I saw fights break out everywhere. I saw two girls from school viciously attacking each other. Clumps of hair and flesh fell to the ground and drifted away. Closer to town, I saw a police officer sprinting around with a traffic cone on his head. Another was repeatedly banging his head against a solid brick wall.

An ice cream truck sounded, that familiar, happy noise that meant a treat. A woman flagged it down by waving frantically and screeching. The ice cream truck pulled over. The man inside opened his serving hatch and punched her. She fell onto the pavement in a heap while he flung ice cream scoops at her.

Everyone is infected! Everyone!

Violence everywhere I looked. Cruelty too and viciousness.

Why aren't I affected yet? Because I'm the carrier? Is it in the air? Because of me?

Questions I didn't know how to answer tumbled around in my head. I stuck to shadows and alleyways as much as I could.

When I got to the park, a mob had tangled our shopkeeper up in one of the chain swings. They were binding him tightly and pushing him. He squealed in pain and fear.

The mob soon grew bored of their cruel game. They descended on the poor shopkeeper and tore him to pieces. Gore and blood flew into the air in their frenzy. They reminded me of the sharks myself and Nina had seen in a documentary. One little child ran off with an ankle and foot, bloody bone poking out of the top.

I covered my mouth and closed my eyes.

This is all my fault. I did this. Me. Everyone's dying because of me.

I felt broken inside. Broken for leaving Nina, my parent's death, and the fact no one believed me.

Hidden in the tree line, I saw a man in a military uniform jog down the street. He launched a flaming bottle with a rag inside at the hairdressers. Fire exploded. The horde, mesmerized by the sudden light, moved as one towards it.

I saw my chance. I ran for the tunnel.

I was meters away when a girl came out of nowhere and slammed into my side. The knife I had clasped tightly in my hand fell away.

Fingernails scraped at my face, blow after blow rained down. She screamed in fury while I kicked out, trying to get her off me.

She spat at me, bit me hard.

A sharp pain hit my stomach. I jerked and jolted until she was flung off. I grabbed her bushy hair and slammed her face down onto the grass.

Get up, get up!

I scrambled to my feet. Blood dripped down my body. The girl had stabbed me with my own knife. The pain was brutal, I couldn't tell how bad it was.

A roar made me look up. The horde had seen me, they were coming for me. Racing towards me like a pack of wild animals. Jaws snapping.

I stumbled to the tunnel and in.

I left behind pools of blood as I walked. The red on metal looked familiar, but I couldn't place it. My mind spasmed. My stomach burned like fire. I clung to the sides of the tunnel and walked, determined to save Nina.

Please let me make it, please. I can warn us. I'm strong, I can do this.

I saw the opening, I saw sunlight. Hope ignited inside me. I gritted my teeth and pushed forward.

Almost there, almost there.

Black spots burst across my vision. Dizziness engulfed me. My movements slowed, my breathing became jagged.

My feet hit the stream, cold water rushed beside me.

Yes! I made it, I made it. Now, I just need to find myself or find Nina.

I looked at the sun, our beautiful sun. I could hear birds chirping, encouraging me on.

The front of my body was drenched in blood.

Keep going, keep going. Am I going to die? Here, now?

It was then that I realized. A cold bolt of horror overwhelmed me.

I was the body they found by the sewer. It was me, my body.

None of this is possible! It's a loop. A circle like our old hula hoops.

Fury raged inside me. I felt the sudden urge to destroy everything and everyone. I wanted to tear and rip. Kill and maim. The feeling was brand new.

A brief thought sparked. Knowledge that I wasn't behaving like myself.

"NO!" I screamed. One final act of defiance before I fell.

They came for us, I came for them, they came for me. I've killed everyone. What have I done!

Coldness spilled into me. Despair and rage. My mind grew tired, thoughts scrambled. I closed my eyes, saw the face of my wonderful friend in my mind. "Nina," I gasped. I held my head in my hands and dropped.

Down into the water, dead.